A CRUSH FOR Christmas

A *Crush* NOVEL

ELOUISE EAST

 Created with Vellum

CONTENTS

Chapter 1	1
Chapter 2	11
Chapter 3	21
Chapter 4	32
Chapter 5	43
Chapter 6	54
Chapter 7	65
Chapter 8	76
Chapter 9	87
Chapter 10	98
Chapter 11	109
Chapter 12	120
Chapter 13	129
Chapter 14	140
Chapter 15	150
Chapter 16	160
About Elouise East	173
Books by Elouise East	175

A CRUSH FOR CHRISTMAS

CHAPTER ONE

COLTON

2017

"Which one are you gonna pick, Dani?"

Jimmy's low, Southern drawl vibrated through Colton Jenkins's body as packed together as they were in the heaving bar. He rolled his eyes at their juvenile game but waited for her answer, nonetheless.

"I'm looking at those two. I'm calling them 'Suit' and 'Red.'" Dani chuckled as she pointed her finger towards the bar at a tall, muscular guy wearing a suit that appeared to be moulded to his body, and then to a slightly smaller, less muscly man about ten feet away from them. The smaller one wore a dark red shirt, but that was all Colton could see.

"No way!" Jimmy answered. "There's no way on God's green earth they will be up for a threesome."

Dani turned her face to Jimmy, eyebrow raised. "And why the hell not?"

Jimmy glanced back over at the guys, and his forehead creased as he shook his head. "I just don't see it."

She twisted to Colton. "What do you think?"

He waved his hand dismissively. "I'm staying out of it."

"Colton!" Dani whined. When all he did was stare at her, she huffed and turned back to Jimmy. "What about you?"

"Easy," Jimmy said with a grin. "Those two." He lifted his chin to indicate the table right in front of them where two women sat, staring at Jimmy while holding their straws to their mouths.

"Fuck, Jimmy. That's cheating."

"What did I do?"

Their squabbling continued, but Colton tuned it out. Every night out was the same, although the results differed. They chose two people—guys for Dani, any gender for Jimmy—to see if they could persuade them to have a threesome. Colton would give them some points for being completely up front with the people involved— not about the game but about it being just one night, not a long-term investment.

Dani had been hurt before by asshole boyfriends and was a lot more cautious now. She shied away from any kind of relationship that lasted longer than a night, and thankfully, in some ways, New York had plenty of people to choose from.

Jimmy, on the other hand, was in love with his boss. Head over heels, completely, totally besotted. He'd been hired by a company as a personal assistant to one of the managers and had been working there for three years before the manager left, leaving Vanessa in their stead. Jimmy had fallen hard but refused to say a word, not wanting to lose his job, understandably. Due to that, he played hard when he wasn't working. Colton wished Jimmy would take a chance one day and explain to Vanessa exactly what he was feeling. Jimmy would be pleasantly surprised if Colton's gut instinct was any indication. He'd only seen her a few times, but she seemed genuine enough.

As for him, he wanted it all—love, marriage, kids, the whole shebang. He hadn't been able to find anyone that made his heart leap, though. His instinct was surprisingly quiet when it came to his own love life.

He lifted his beer and swallowed some of the lukewarm liquid, grimacing as he gazed around the dimly lit room. Beer should only be ice cold, in his opinion. Colton scratched at the scruff on his jaw, knowing it needed to be trimmed soon. When it grew longer than three days' worth, it began to look unkempt. He didn't worry as much when he was working the stalls in the winter because it kept him warmer as he stood selling his stock to tourists and locals alike in the freezing temperatures of New York City. Luckily, he also had decent clothes to keep the chill from invading his bones.

Union Square Holiday Market had been a good choice again so far. Although he always had to finish earlier than when it ended on Christmas Eve, he didn't mind at all. Seeing his mother was more important, even if she was over three thousand miles away from him at the moment.

"What do you think?"

Colton tuned back in to the conversation, staring blankly at Jimmy. "What?" He glanced back and forth between his two best friends, mentally acknowledging that if Jimmy hadn't been in love with Vanessa, he and Dani would make a really good couple.

Jimmy sighed and pursed his lips. "Weren't you listening?"

"Nope." Colton didn't see the point in denying it.

"Do you want to get out of here?"

Colton raised his eyebrows. "What about your conquests?"

Dani shook her head. "I can't be bothered tonight, to be honest." She drained her glass of wine before reaching forward to place it on the bar between two patrons who were standing there. Dragging her coat on, she crossed her arms and tapped her foot. Patience had never been one of her virtues.

Snorting, Colton excused himself to a woman as he put his unfinished beer down next to her, then offered his elbow to Dani. "Your chariot awaits, my lady," he said with a grin. "Come on, bucko," he added, peering over his shoulder at Jimmy, whose face had fallen as he stared at the two women from earlier.

"Fine." Jimmy's petulant tone had Colton sniggering as he guided Dani through the rowdy throng to the exit.

Dani shuddered, as did he when the cold bite of the wind invaded the gaps in his clothing, sending goosebumps along Colton's skin. He buttoned his coat, turning his collar up against the frigid air and wrapped his arm around Dani as they walked to the subway.

They had met at that bar because it was close to the

market. He hadn't had any plans to find a hookup, so hadn't changed before meeting them. Although his clothes were good, they didn't keep all the cold out. Dani would be frozen if they didn't get her home quickly. As per their routine, all three trudged to the train before Colton waved goodbye to them both and made his own way home.

Finally arriving at the place he called his, Colton dropped his keys onto the kitchen counter and sighed. He loved his little one-bed apartment, but he'd always hoped for more. Since his father had died ten years ago, he'd been alone in New York. His mother had decided, not long after, she couldn't stand being in the busy city a moment longer, despite being a New Yorker born and bred, and had emigrated across the Atlantic to the UK where his dad's family lived. Colton didn't blame her. There was nothing in the Big Apple for her, except him. All of his mother's family had passed years before, so there was nothing holding her there any longer.

Colton refused to give up his home. He wanted to make things work in the city where his parents had chosen to raise him. Times were hard, and many a night, he'd eaten noodles or such like to make sure he could afford the rent that month. He was pleased to note, he had never missed a payment. Things were difficult, though, and something needed to change if he wanted to continue doing what he loved.

Glancing over at the small pile of wood in front of his window, he smiled. It wasn't much but being able to afford decent wood to create the trinkets and gifts he sold was pleasing. He spent much of his free time working with the wood to make keychains, pens, toys, decorations, small boxes, candle holders and much more. His market stall was his pride and joy, all the stock being handmade by him.

Colton's smile faded a little as he thought about the need for more income. Rent was rising, as always, and he needed to figure out what he was going to do.

After sending a text to Dani and Jimmy telling them he was home, he warmed up his noodles and sat on the lone sofa, thinking about his upcoming trip. Every year since she'd moved, Colton visited his mother in the UK at Christmas. It wasn't just because it was Christmas, but also because her birthday was the day after. Unfortunately, due to costs, Colton could only stay for a week. He hated leaving her each time, but she was happy, and he couldn't wish for more.

The previous year, she had moved into a nursing home. She was only sixty-five, but she had insisted, in one of her lucid moments, that everyone stop worrying over her and let her stay somewhere she would not be a burden. The whole family had rallied at that, but she had put her foot down, and that had been it. Colton had not been there to see the move, but last Christmas, he had visited the nursing home and been overwhelmed by how nice it and all the staff were.

They had welcomed him as if they knew him, and when he'd asked, they'd explained his mother had been talking about him non-stop, so it felt like they had met him already.

It had been difficult to see her there, but Colton knew it had been the best decision. His mother had lupus—or systemic lupus erythematosus—which basically meant her immune system attacked the healthy parts of her body by mistake. It caused inflammation to her joints, rashes and a whole dictionary full of different symptoms that made her life difficult. It wasn't called the 'disease of a thousand faces' for nothing.

The worst thing for Colton was the memory issues. Whenever his mother had a flare-up, her memory was one of the first things to show it. She would stare at an object or person, uncomprehending who or what it was. She would forget how to do the simplest of tasks, like how to flush the toilet or how to switch on the TV. It broke his heart to see her that way, especially when there was no cure.

Shaking his head, he thrust away his maudlin thoughts and focused on what he needed to do before he flew to be with her. He had just over a month before his flight, and there was something special he wanted to make her.

With Jimmy and Dani's help, he packed up his stall at the end of his season and made sure everything fit into the little van he'd hired for the evening. It was an expense he hated paying out for but a necessary one because there was no way he'd be able to cart everything to his apartment. He knew from experience. The first year, he'd used a large trolley to pull his stock to and from his apartment. Never again.

After they unloaded the boxes and trudged them all the way up to the second floor, they collapsed, gasping for breath.

"Jesus, Colton. You have got to get a ground floor apartment. This shit is a killer," Jimmy stated as he lay spread eagle on the floor.

Colton leaned against the wall, legs spread as he recovered. Jimmy was right, but he had no choice. At least, it kept him fit without the need for a gym membership.

"It's takeout night," Dani declared. "My treat."

"You don't need—"

"Shut up," she said without heat. "You're not here for Christmas, so this will be our Christmas meal." She didn't move from her position of resting her head on Jimmy's stomach as she dialled for Chinese.

Colton felt bad that he couldn't help out with the cost of the takeaway, but all his money had been sunk into the flight and hotel. He wished he'd been able to stay at his uncle's place; however, they had a three-bedroom house with all the bedrooms full of kids. When he'd visited last year, he had used some extra money to reserve a room at a small hotel chain. Luckily, it was closer to his mother's nursing home than his uncle's house.

As they ate chicken chow mein, duck pancakes and beef satay, they talked about what Jimmy's and Dani's plans were, then decided what the three of them were doing for New Year's Eve. Dani had insisted on the ritual of New Year because Colton wasn't with them for Christmas, and he hadn't had the heart to tell her he hated the celebration.

"I'm heading home." Dani lifted herself from the floor with a groan. "My muscles are never going to forgive you, Geppetto."

Colton snorted at the nickname Dani called him on occasion, usually when she was hurling insults. Problem was, he didn't mind being thrown in with the man who had made a wooden boy.

"You'll survive, Dee," he retorted with his own nickname, knowing she hated the shortened version.

"Fuck you." She saluted him with her middle finger before hauling him in for a hug. "Take care and say hello to your mom for me." Dani kissed him on the cheek and pulled away.

"Well, another year, another flight. Are you ever going to move over there?"

It was a question Jimmy asked every year, and every year, Colton's answer was the same, "My home is here."

Jimmy nodded slowly, then dragged him closer, wrapping his arms around him. "Gonna miss you, Colt."

Colton swallowed hard. He knew what Jimmy meant. It was just as difficult for him not to be with part of his family—as he thought of Jimmy and Dani—as it was for them, even though they had blood family to celebrate with.

"Safe flight."

Locking the door behind them, Colton rested his forehead against the painted wood and closed his eyes. His emotions were all mixed up between joy that he'd see his mother and sadness that he wouldn't see Jimmy and

Dani. But he only saw his mother once a year, so his friends would have to wait.

He threw himself into finishing his packing, setting his alarm for his god-awful early flight, and crashed.

By the time he had arrived at the hotel in Cambridge, he was exhausted. He dragged his two suitcases into the room and let it slam behind him, wincing and silently apologising to anyone who was asleep, despite it being early evening in the UK. He dropped onto the bed and stared at the ceiling. He'd dragged himself out of bed at two-thirty that morning to catch his 6 a.m. flight and was glad for it because it meant his jet lag wouldn't, hopefully, be as bad as normal.

With the UK being five hours ahead of New York, Colton had basically lost a day due to travelling. But he was determined to make sure his tiredness didn't interfere with seeing his mother. At that thought, he picked himself up and headed for a shower.

CHAPTER TWO

IOAN

Ioan Thomas rolled his head, trying to ease the ache in his neck he'd woken up with that morning. He'd groaned when his alarm had gone off at five, and he'd rolled over in pain, but a hot shower had loosened it some.

"Ioan, have you been in to see Rose yet?" Laura, the manager of Cambridge Nursing Home, asked.

"No. It's my next stop."

"I bet she'll be so excited to see her son today."

Ioan chuckled. "She'll probably be dancing in the hallways until he arrives."

Laura laughed as she carried on past him towards her office, and Ioan headed to Rose's room, knocking before entering. "Good morning, Rose. How are you feeling today?"

"Ioan." The happy greeting that met him was a balm to his soul. Another good day for Mrs Jenkins, hopefully. "I'm feeling very excited, Ioan. CJ should be here soon."

"I know, Rose. He'll be here before you know it." Ioan patted her hand. "Shall we get you up and out of bed, and you can greet him with all your bells and whistles on."

Rose tittered. "I'm getting a little old for bells and whistles, Ioan, but getting dressed would be great."

They went through their usual routine, Ioan helping Rose to get to the bathroom so she could clean herself while he busied himself making her bed and tidying away anything that didn't need to be out. When she shuffled back into the room, he helped her to dress. Once she was situated in her favourite armchair in front of the TV, Ioan left to get her breakfast. Some residents preferred to eat their first meal alone.

As he sauntered back to her room, carrying her breakfast tray, he heard a distinctive accent behind him, and a shiver went down his spine. Ioan paused, twisting slightly to observe the man at the reception desk. The spiky, sandy blond hair and three-day scruff had not changed in the year since Ioan last saw Colton and, when Colton faced him, neither had the spark that lit in his chest whenever their gazes met.

Ignoring his reaction, he said, "Mr Jenkins? Your mum is this way." His heart missed a beat when Colton —not CJ as his mother called him, that was reserved just for her—grinned at him.

"Ioan. Nice to see you again. I wasn't sure if the staff would've changed since I was last here."

"We are quite good at keeping our staff, it seems," Ioan said, continuing to walk while trying to ignore Colton's nearness.

"I'm glad. I'd hate to have to remember new people's names every time I came back." Colton chuckled. "How is she?"

"She's having a good day and is so excited to see you. She's sat watching TV while I fetched her breakfast. We weren't expecting you for another hour or so."

Colton flushed, and Ioan tried to wet his dry throat. "I was excited," he said quietly.

"I can imagine. Good thing you have special visiting times, eh?"

Laura had sat down with Colton the previous year to discuss his plans for while he was there. They had agreed for the duration of his visit that he could visit his mother whenever he wanted to as long as he didn't disturb the other residents. Colton had agreed, so he was able to come and go as he pleased. The previous year, he had been mostly at the nursing home during the day, except when his mum had a nap, then he walked the grounds.

Ioan had been impressed with how devoted Colton had been, and when they had found time for a chat, Ioan had found out some more about the situation surrounding their close-knit family. It had turned out, they had a similar family situation. Colton only had his mum left; Ioan only had his dad. Neither had siblings, and both had extended family that they didn't see very much. They were also a similar age, although Ioan had two years on Colton.

Ioan entered Rose's room, placing the tray on the little wooden table they used as her dining table when she was in her room. "I found a stranger out in the corridor. Should I let him keep you company?"

Rose frowned at him, then the creases on her forehead cleared when she saw Colton, and a radiant smile spread across her face.

Colton stepped towards her as she rose out of her chair, wrapping his arms around her and burying his face in her neck. Ioan heard sniffling and moved his gaze away from the private moment, wiping his finger under his eyes to remove the evidence of his own tears. Emotional reunions always made him teary. He concentrated on laying out Rose's breakfast, waiting until they had started talking before glancing over to check if they were still embraced. When he saw they weren't, he picked the table up and carried it to next to the chair.

"Your breakfast is served, madam," he said in a posh accent and with a bow, just like a butler in one of her favourite movies. He glanced at Colton, lifting the back of his hand to shield his mouth from Rose in a pretend secret conversation. "There's even some extra strawberries if you'd like some."

Colton grinned at him. "Thanks, Ioan."

"I'll leave you to your food. Give me a shout if you need anything; otherwise, I will see you in a little while."

"Thank you, Ioan," Rose said with a smile.

"You're very welcome, my dear."

Ioan smiled at Colton once more before leaving the room. He inhaled deeply as he walked away from the room, trying to push away the feelings that Colton always seemed to bring out in him. He'd thought it was a one-off last year that every time he saw Colton, his heart rate increased. He'd also thought this year would be different because he'd not seen him for twelve months. Obviously, he'd been mistaken, which was going to be awkward unless he could get his feelings under control for the next few days.

The rest of the morning was filled with his usual routine of taking care of several of the residents and supervising the games session in the large living area. The residents had a choice of joining other residents in games, like backgammon or cards, or sitting and watching a film, which today was *Miracle on 34th Street*. He hadn't seen or heard from Rose and Colton, so he assumed they were still catching up.

After the residents' lunch, the staff helped each of them back to their rooms for their afternoon nap or quiet time if they didn't want to sleep. It was usually the time when visitors went home.

Ioan strode towards Rose's room, knocking gently before entering after he was invited to. "Hey. I wanted to check if you were feeling a little sleepy, Rose. I thought all this excitement might have worn you out."

He studied her as he came closer, noticing the strain on her face, though she tried to hide it.

"Actually, I think I could do with a nap." She glanced at Colton. "Sorry, CJ."

Colton leaned forward, grasping her hands in his and bringing them up to his mouth for a kiss. "Don't be sorry, Mom. I'm not going anywhere. You get some rest, and I'll grab some lunch. When you wake up, I'll come back."

Rose's face lit up at his words, and she removed a hand from Colton's and cupped his jaw. "My precious boy." She kissed his cheek, then let go, peering back at

Ioan. "Sleepytime, as I used to say to CJ when he was little."

"You'll feel much more refreshed after a nap. You'll be able to keep up with your son better."

She chuckled. "I haven't been able to keep up with that boy since he was born."

All three of them laughed as Rose headed to her bed. Ioan helped get her situated and moved into the hallway so Colton could say goodbye. When Colton exited and closed the door quietly, Ioan took in the stress on his face.

"Are you okay, Colton?"

Colton sighed and rubbed a hand over his face. "I hate this. I hate having such a short time with her." He smiled half-heartedly at Ioan. "But she loves it here, which makes it easier to leave." He shook his head. "Three thousand miles is a long way away from family."

Ioan squeezed Colton's shoulder in camaraderie. "I can imagine it is. I'm two hundred and fifty away from my dad, and that's enough for me." He slid his hand off Colton's shoulder for no other reason than he wanted to keep it there. "Tell you what, I'm heading for lunch now. Would you like to join me?"

Colton raised his eyebrows. "Are you sure? I don't want to intrude on your downtime."

Ioan chuckled. "You won't be. I'm just going to head to a bakery near here if you're interested? It's only a five-minute drive."

Colton grimaced. "I'm afraid I don't have a car. Thanks for the invite, though."

Ioan could see that Colton wanted to join him, so extended an offer he didn't think he'd ever get over if it was accepted. "Well, we can walk. It'll take about fifteen minutes or I have my bike here. If you don't mind holding onto me, you're welcome to have a lift." His heart raced as he waited for Colton's answer.

"Motorcycle?" At Ioan's nod, Colton grinned. "I'd love to! I've never been on one, but I've always wanted to try it."

Ioan beamed, though his heart cracked at the joy crossing Colton's face. Such a small thing for Ioan to do, but such excitement from Colton. "Come on, then." Ioan strode down the hallway, signing out at reception after he'd retrieved his jacket and bag. He had an hour before he had to be back.

They shuffled out into the cold air, pulling their coats closer before stopping at Ioan's bike. The sleek black motorbike had been his first independent purchase, and it was his pride and joy.

"Wow. What model is this?" Colton asked as he walked around it, staring at the vehicle.

"It's a Kawasaki Ninja. The bike I wanted for ages." Ioan grinned as he pulled the helmets free. Luckily, he always kept a spare with him and passed it over to Colton. "Do you know how to put it on?" Colton smiled and, without answering, slipped it on and fastened it. "Okay." Ioan laughed and pulled his helmet on before swinging his leg over, settling himself into the seat. "Hold on to me as you climb on," he told Colton.

Ioan held the bike steady as Colton got settled. He'd had people on the back of his bike before, but since it was being Colton, he was a little more hesitant, especially as it was Colton who had to wrap his arms around his waist.

"Hold onto me." Ioan started the engine, the rumbling purr vibrating through his body, centring him more than anything else. At least, until Colton's arms slid around his waist and his back moulded to him. Ioan inhaled shakily. "You ready?"

"All set."

The helmets had built-in microphones, so there was no need to shout to each other. They could have a normal conversation if they wanted to. As Ioan pulled out of the car park and onto the main road, Colton's arms tightened, making Ioan wish the ride was a lot longer than five minutes.

When they arrived at the bakery, Ioan turned off the bike before indicating for Colton to climb off. He set the stand, then swung his leg over. As Colton removed his helmet, Ioan's breath escaped in a rush at the huge, unrestrained smile and laugh that came from Colton.

"That was amazing!"

Ioan snorted. "That was only five minutes." He secured the helmets and pointed over his shoulder. "Here's the bakery."

The bell over the door tinkled as they entered, and the scent of freshly baked goods had Ioan smiling. Nothing beats a sandwich made from warm bread straight from the oven. He waved at Audrey behind the till and went to find a table. They hooked their coats on the back of their chairs before sitting.

"A new baker started here a couple of months ago,

and his food is to die for." Ioan chuckled as he picked up the menu. "I think this place gets most of my wages."

Colton grinned. "A place to put on the 'must visit' list whenever I come, then."

"Definitely. I'll go bankrupt coming here."

"Blame Theo for that, Ioan, not me," Audrey joked as she stopped by their table.

"I blame all of you. I have to visit the gym more often because of you lot."

Audrey chuckled. "What can I get you?"

"A mocha for me, please. Colton?"

"Do you have a spiced pumpkin latte?"

Audrey smiled. "My American friend, why, yes, we do. New to us this year, in fact."

"Great. Yes, please."

"Wonderful. I'll grab your drinks and take your order when I come back."

"Thanks, Audrey," Ioan said. "Latte, pumpkins and spices? Seriously?" The idea did not sound at all tasty.

"Don't knock it until you've tried it." Colton smirked.

"Hmm, I don't think so."

After Audrey deposited their drinks and took their food order, Colton asked, "So, where does your dad live if you're over two hundred miles away from him?"

"He lives in North Wales."

"Is that where you're originally from?" Colton asked.

"No, we lived in Kent when I was born. Dad owned a bar for many years, but when he realised I had no interest in taking over from him, he decided to sell up and retire. With the money he received, he moved back to his hometown of Caernarfon."

"Did you not want to move with him?"

"I had already been accepted at Cambridge University when he made the decision." Ioan shrugged. "I might have changed where I'd planned to go if I'd known before. Or maybe not, I don't know. I love where I am now. Nothing can make me move at the moment."

"It's nice to have a job you enjoy doing, isn't it?"

"It is. I especially love it when the residents get excited about their visitors." Ioan grinned. "Whenever I'm told of your arrival date, I make sure to countdown for your mother. The closer it gets, the more excited she is."

"Me, too." Colton reached across the table and rested his hand on Ioan's. "Thank you for doing that. It goes above and beyond your job description."

Ioan felt his cheeks heat, and he stared at his mocha. He had to keep hold of his emotions. There was no way he was starting anything that would end up being long-distance. And anyway, Colton probably wasn't even gay. Rose had certainly never said one way or the other.

CHAPTER THREE

COLTON

Colton had been lucky with his mom. She'd had a good couple of days, and it had almost made him forget. Until he walked into the nursing home and saw Ioan's face.

"She's not having such a good day today, I'm afraid."

Colton exhaled slowly and closed his eyes. He hated that she had these episodes. More so that there was no way of preventing or predicting them.

"Are you okay?" Ioan's voice penetrated his thoughts.

Colton forced a smile. "Yeah. It just…sucks. You know?"

Ioan rubbed a hand on Colton's back. "I know." And Colton knew he did. Ioan must see it day in, day out.

Bracing himself, he strolled towards his mother's room, knocking gently and peering around the door before entering.

"Hey, Mom." He wandered over to her bed where she was propped up, staring at the TV. She slowly moved her head to look at him. Seeing no recognition in her expression, he bit his lip to hold back the tears.

"Hello."

She continued to look at him, so he pulled a chair closer and sat next to her, clearing his throat.

"What are you watching?"

"I'm watching…" she trailed off, returning her gaze to the TV but frowning at it.

When she didn't continue, Colton said, "It looks like a Christmas movie to me." She didn't reply, and he didn't expect her to. They spent an hour or so watching the film, during which Colton had a one-sided conversation with her. He'd been told by a doctor once that although his mom didn't reply, she was listening, even if she didn't understand everything that was said. It had given him the confidence to keep talking regardless of any response.

His mother began to get restless, so he called for a nurse. Ioan entered and immediately began chatting to her and getting her ready for a nap. Colton just watched from the sidelines as Ioan did what he did whenever Colton wasn't there. After Rose was settled, Colton went over and pressed a kiss to her forehead. "Love you, Mom."

By late afternoon, his mother had begun to become more lucid, although not by much. At least, she was able to identify Colton, even if she didn't understand why he was there. By dinner time, he couldn't take anymore, and although he felt awful, he said goodbye to everyone and left.

Returning to his hotel, he had a shower, then dressed in his nicest jeans and a button-down shirt, grabbed his keys, phone and wallet and headed out the door. Crush was his destination. He'd found the bar by chance when he'd been wandering the streets of Cambridge during his stay a couple of years prior. It was a lovely little pub that sold local and national beers, and Colton had instantly felt at home. Since then, he made sure to visit each time he was in Cambridge.

As he entered, he noticed the interior hadn't changed much since the previous year. He assumed the bartenders would be different, so he was surprised to be greeted by Analise and Rob, the same staff that had been there before.

"How are you doing?" Colton asked Analise when she poured him a drink.

"Alright, thanks. God, I will never tire of hearing your accent." She laughed as she placed his beer in front of him. "Feel free to talk nonsense to me all night." She winked and collected his payment.

Colton chuckled, knowing she didn't want anything more than friendship. They'd had that conversation when they'd first met. Rob was more stoic, nodding at him, but they didn't have the same friendship as he had with Analise.

Shifting his head back and forth to release the tension in his neck, he blew out a breath. He just needed to let off some steam.

"That's a neat keychain. Can I ask where you bought it?" A voice next to him snapped his gaze to the side.

A tall, slim guy perched on a seat one over from him, and Colton studied him quickly. The guy had long brown hair with blond highlights tucked up into a ponytail and a similar style beard to his own. He had a large forehead with lines showing the laughter present in his life. His eyes shone under Colton's perusal, and he flushed.

"Sorry. Just deciding if you were a serial killer or not," he joked, trying to mask his embarrassment.

"No problem. I can assure you I'm not, but that won't help you, I'm sure." The guy smiled and held out his hand. "Zak King. These pair can vouch for me if needed." He indicated Analise and Rob with a tilt of his head.

"I'm not telling anyone I know you. My reputation would be ruined," Analise teased, smirking.

"You wound me, oh fair one!" Zak laughed before turning back to Colton. "Can I have a look?"

Colton wondered what Zak was talking about until he pointed at his keychain. "Sure."

Zak picked it up and studied the wooden carving Colton had made about five years ago. It was an intricate piece, detailing ropes intertwining into a knot, and it was his favourite.

"This is fantastic workmanship. Where did you buy it?"

"I didn't. I made it." Colton cleared his throat and gulped down some beer, hating his uncertainty when showing off his work.

Zak raised his eyebrows, the creases in his forehead deepening. "Seriously?" At Colton's nod, Zak whistled. "I hope you sell these."

Colton's mouth quirked up. "Yeah, and a few other pieces. I have a stall back in New York, and I follow where the markets are throughout the year."

Zak huffed a laugh. "I'm a woodworker, too."

"Really?" It was Colton's turn to be surprised, not that Zak worked with wood, but that they'd managed to find someone who did the same job but lived an ocean apart.

"Yeah. I started my business a few years ago and have been slowly gaining more customers and custom piece requests. I mainly work with furniture, although I do make smaller items as gifts for friends and family."

"Huh. What're the chances?"

For the rest of the evening, Colton and Zak swapped stories about what they made and how their businesses worked, and Colton was introduced to several of Zak's friends. When Colton couldn't keep his eyes open any longer, he bid goodnight and headed back to the hotel. Zak had given him some brilliant ideas for how to expand what he already sold and to make customised items, too. He'd taken Zak's phone number when it was offered, in case he had any ideas or questions or needed a sounding board. He didn't think he'd ever use it, but it was nice to have the option.

As he settled into bed, he stared at the ceiling, thinking about what had happened. His mother had been right in insisting on living at the nursing home. Despite how much it hurt to have her surrounded by strangers—at least strangers at the time, not now—he realised his uncle wouldn't have been able to look after her when she had days like that. If he was honest, he wasn't sure *he* would've been able to manage to take care of her like Ioan and the staff did. Ioan, especially, was amazing with her.

A message sounded on his phone, and he reached over to pick it up from the bedside table.

How are you, Geppetto?

Dani's message made him chuckle, but he didn't want to burden her with his depressing thoughts, so he put his phone back and turned over. He would answer her tomorrow.

Christmas Day dawned bright and early, at least for Colton. His mother had been a lot better the previous day and would, hopefully, be feeling back to normal for one of their special days together. Colton was so excited to see her, but he wasn't going to turn up at the crack of dawn just because he couldn't sleep. The residents were probably still snoozing.

He checked his bag to make sure he had everything he needed to spend the day at the nursing home, including some gifts for the staff to show his appreciation, especially as some had to forgo their own family celebrations to take care of the residents.

When the time was the better side of suitable, he grabbed his things and headed out. The chilly morning temperature reminded him of New York, and he marched through it without issue, too intent on his destination.

Thirty minutes later, and with a nose as red as a certain reindeer, he entered the nursing home. Before he visited with his mother, he left the general presents at the reception desk. He had bought enough chocolate for the staff to enjoy. The only person who had a specific gift was Ioan. Colton felt nervous about giving it to Ioan because Colton had made it specially for him. He hadn't known at the time why he felt the need to make this particular item, but he couldn't help the feeling. So, he had made it and wrapped it, thinking he probably wouldn't even get up the nerve to give it to Ioan in the end.

Knocking on his mother's door, he entered slowly so he didn't disturb her if she was still asleep. She wasn't. She stood, staring out of the window, wringing her hands together.

"Mom?"

Rose spun around with a huge smile on her face and rushed across the floor, wrapping her arms around Colton. With a chuckle, he did the same.

"Happy Christmas, sweetheart." His mother pulled back and cupped his face in her hands. "You look more grown-up every time I see you."

Colton rolled his eyes. "Mom! I'm thirty-five. I'm not sure how much more grown-up I can look."

"You'll always be my baby, CJ, no matter how old you get." Rose patted his cheek and let go. "Did you see the little tree?" She pointed to the corner of the room where a three-foot plastic tree with integrated lights had been decorated sparsely but tastefully.

Colton's heart jumped a little, knowing the tree had

been placed there the day she'd not been feeling well, and she obviously couldn't remember. "I bet that was a nice surprise for you," he said with a grin, holding back his emotions as best he could.

"It was. It's so lovely. The reds and golds look wonderful together, and it's so sparkly when the lights are off." She gently touched the tree as if scared she would knock it over, then turned to him with a smile. "I'm so glad you're here. Are you staying for lunch?"

Colton grinned. "I'm here all day. You'll never get rid of me." He paused. "I did wonder if you'd like to visit Uncle Brian before lunch. If we headed over there now, we would have time to see the kids open some of their presents, then we'd be back here in time for lunch. What do you think?"

The choice was left to her because, although she was fond of his dad's family, she was often over-whelmed by the number of people when they all got together.

"I'd like that."

"Okay. Let me clear it with the staff, and I'll be back in a few minutes."

Colton headed down the corridor towards the reception desk.

"Merry Christmas, Colton."

Ioan's voice stopped him in his tracks, and he spun around before chuckling. "Nice hat." He grinned. "Merry Christmas, Ioan. I didn't expect you to be here today." He wasn't sure why he hadn't expected him to be, but for some reason, he just hadn't.

Ioan shrugged. "I always work Christmas Day. I don't

have any family here, so I let someone else who does have the day with theirs. It's the least I can do."

"Wouldn't you go and visit your dad?"

"I could, but he always makes plans to meet up with his friends. I don't want him to stop that just because I visit him. I go and see him for New Year instead."

Colton nodded. With the gold-coloured tinsel wrapped around his head as a halo, Ioan's eyes seemed brighter, a shinier brandy colour than usual. His jet-black hair looked expertly tousled beneath the golden ring, with small waves curling around the edges of his ears.

When he realised he'd been staring, Colton cleared his throat. "Um…oh, I was wondering if it was okay to take Mom to see Uncle Brian for an hour or so?" He changed the subject, not wanting to think about his reaction to Ioan.

"Of course. All you need to do is sign her out. Lunch will be for one o'clock just so you know."

"Thanks. We'll be back before then. Uncle Brian's is a madhouse." Colton chuckled.

Ioan grinned. "Ah, so you'll be coming back here for a rest."

"Definitely. We may just crash and burn after spending an hour with potentially twenty people, if not more."

"Wow. Not sure I could deal with that either."

Colton's gaze dropped to Ioan's mouth as he spoke, the full lips that curved into a grin when he was happy, and the lines bracketing that smile showed years of joy and laughter—at least he hoped that's what it meant.

"Um…okay, we'll get ourselves ready and sign out

before we go. Thanks." Colton backed away down the corridor towards his mother's room again, needing to gain some distance. He gave a small wave and fled.

He'd never looked at Ioan in such detail before, and he wondered why, suddenly, he had begun to. Shaking off his thoughts, he entered his mother's room, remembering he hadn't given her his gift yet.

"I have something for you." The largest of the gifts was removed from the bag he'd brought with him and placed on the bed. "Merry Christmas, Mom."

"Oh, CJ, you didn't have to do that." Rose moved over to the bed and reverently ran her hands over the paper.

"You can open it, you know," Colton remarked with a smile.

"I'm savouring it," his mother chided.

She peeled off some of the tape holding it together, memories of previous years coming to the forefront of Colton's mind. Rose always tried to save the paper, saying it could be used again. One year, Colton had suggested they just rip it off and see what happens, but his mother had gasped in horror, and he'd never suggested it again.

Licking his lips, he waited in anticipation of the unveiling, hoping she liked what he'd made.

"Oh, my word! That is amazing! Did you make that?"

"Yeah."

The wooden structure was a replication of a stable in miniature form. Once his mother had opened the rest of the small gifts that came with it, there would be figures that could be placed inside the space Colton had left for them. It was the most detailed piece he had ever made, and he loved how it had turned out. Although his mother wasn't religious, she had always loved the story behind the imagery.

After they had found a place for the stable to fit and his mother had opened the remaining gifts, they climbed into the taxi aimed for his uncle's house. He had been right when he'd spoken to Ioan, there were around twenty people at the house, and the place was in utter chaos. When they were finally sat in the living room with the rest of the family, ten children began unwrapping and screeching at the gifts they'd been given. As much as he loved his father's family, they were definitely over-whelming in large doses, but he loved them all the same.

CHAPTER FOUR

IOAN

Ioan blew out a breath when all of the residents, barring one, were seated at small round tables in the dining hall with their families. Larger round tables were placed intermittently between them for the residents who didn't have any family visiting that day or for residents with only one family member, like Rose. At least one member of staff would be sitting at each of those larger tables so the residents could feel comfortable during the meal.

Christmas had never really been his favourite celebration. Ioan always preferred birthdays, but for a lot of people, the December festivities were important, and he loved making things as beautiful and exciting as possible for them. He hadn't hesitated when Laura had asked him to organise it that year.

"Sorry, we got side-tracked. We're not late, are we?" Colton entered the room with Rose by his side.

"No, not at all. I've seated you over here." Ioan's

pulse increased as he showed them where to sit. He would be at the same table as them, and he needed to remember not to stare at Colton all day. His thoughts had repeatedly veered towards the American since Colton had arrived, more so than usual, and Ioan wasn't quite sure what to do about it if anything.

After checking to make sure everyone had everything they needed, Ioan headed to the kitchen to let the staff know everything was ready to start. He returned to his seat and started a conversation with John, an older man who had no living family members. Their conversation turned to his younger years and what he remembered of his parents and their celebrations as the food was delivered.

Every person had been given coloured paper hats if they wanted to wear them, but Ioan had forgone the usual party poppers when one resident had become frightened last year once the snapping noise had occurred.

As Ioan looked around the room as the meal wore on, he smiled when he saw smiling faces throughout the dining hall. Though he didn't have any blood relatives here, this was his family.

He caught Colton's gaze and held it as heat raced through his body. Colton was such a good person, which was the only reason Ioan could think to why he was suddenly *more* interested in him—before he'd just found him attractive. He refused to do anything about it. If he couldn't manage a long-distance relationship that was only one hundred miles, there was no way he could do three *thousand* miles. Brushing away the thought of his failed past, he broke his gaze away and concentrated on what Millie was saying about her newest knitting project.

Once dinner was finished, Ioan began helping those residents who needed assistance back to their rooms for their nap. He visited each of those under his care to make sure they had everything they needed, then headed for Rose's room, leaving them until last.

"Knock, knock," he called as he peered around the slightly open door.

"Ioan!" Rose came over to him and hugged him. "I know we were sat at the table together, but Merry Christmas."

"You, too, Rose. Have you had a good day?"

"Yes! Brian and his family had grown even more than I realised. I can't even remember how many grandkids he has now." Rose's eyes radiated joy and happiness.

"It must've been wonderful to see them all."

"It was." She yawned behind her hand. "Oh, sorry. I think I need a nap."

"I'm not surprised. You've been a right social butterfly today." Ioan chuckled. "Let's get you sorted."

He busied around, fetching what Rose needed and helped her to get into bed, making sure there was a fresh glass of water next to her. Colton leaned over and kissed her on her forehead before following Ioan out of the room.

"I think she was asleep before we even closed the door," Colton snorted.

"I agree." Ioan slipped his hands into the pockets of his tunic, suddenly nervous.

"Oh, this is for you." Colton held out a small present.

"You didn't have to—"

"I know, but..." Colton didn't seem to be able to finish, so Ioan didn't push.

"Thank you."

"Okay, I'm going to head to the hotel. After all that food, I think *I* need a nap." Colton grinned.

"Have a nice sleep."

Ioan watched as Colton disappeared down the corridor before focusing on the gift. He pulled the wrapping off, stuffing it into his pocket to dispose of later and held the small wooden object in his palm. The dark-coloured wood—he had no idea what type of wood it was—was polished to perfection. The item was a keychain of his initial, but it has intricate carvings on the whole letter. It almost looked like rose bindings wrapping around the letter, and it was fairly heavy but beautifully made. Ioan glanced up at the space where Colton had disappeared, his heart tumbling over itself.

He was getting in deeper than he should.

The following morning, he made a trip to the nursing home despite it being his day off. It was, after all, Rose's birthday, and he had a gift for her. He waved at Amanda behind reception and carried on down the corridor until he came to Rose's door, where he knocked.

"Come in!" she called.

"Hey, birthday girl. How are you today?"

"I wasn't expecting to see you. I thought you weren't working?" Rose came over and hugged him, rubbing her hand up and down his back as she usually did. Something, he'd noticed, she always did to Colton, too.

"I'm not, but I couldn't forget your birthday now, could I?" He held out his gift. "Happy birthday, Rose."

"Oh, you shouldn't have." Despite her words, she giggled and went over to her chair before beginning to open it.

Ioan lifted his gaze to Colton, seeing him staring at him with a smile. "Morning."

"Good morning." Colton rose from his seat and came to stand next to him as they watched Rose. "You spoil her."

Ioan grinned at him. "Who doesn't deserve a little spoiling every now and then?"

Colton chuckled.

"Oh, my! Ioan, it's beautiful," Rose exclaimed.

Ioan felt his face heat as Colton moved over to his mother, crouching next to her chair and studying the framed photograph he'd had printed. It was a picture of her and Colton on the first day he'd arrived at the nursing home this year. Ioan had managed to snap a picture without them knowing, which he felt bad about, but he excused himself because it was for a present. They were sitting huddled together on a sofa in the living area looking at a book, and their expressions as they glanced at each other were open, loving and beautiful. He hadn't been able to resist and had known there and then what he was going to give her for her birthday.

"Thank you, Ioan." Rose came forward and hugged

him again, and he felt the prickles in the corners of his eyes and swallowed heavily.

"You're very welcome, Rose. Right, I'll leave you to your day, and I'll see you tomorrow."

"Have a good day, Ioan," Colton said quietly.

Their eyes met briefly before Ioan forced himself to look away. He waved goodbye to Amanda and set off home. He could do with getting some more food in the house but couldn't be bothered to deal with all the shoppers who were no doubt already out and about trying to get to the sales.

His phone vibrated as he parked his bike in his driveway, and he pulled it out of his pocket.

Fancy a couple of beers?

He and Kyle had become friends when Ioan had first moved to Cambridge. He'd gone out for a drink, and Kyle had flirted with him. Once they'd realised they weren't right for each other—before they'd had sex, luckily—they'd become best friends instead. Kyle was an electrician and worked as many hours as he could find work for, saving to buy a house for his spouse and children. Not that he was even in a relationship at that moment, but Kyle had a plan, and he was determined to follow it.

As much as he probably could've done with going out and relaxing, he wasn't in the mood.

Maybe another day. I'm knackered.

Not strictly true, but Ioan didn't want to deal with any of the theatrics Kyle usually brought with him.

He locked his bike in the garage and let himself into the house. It was only a small two-bedroom place, but Ioan loved the simplicity of it. He didn't need a big house at the moment, and if he ever did, he would sell this one and buy a new one. Ioan's plans weren't as grand as Kyle's. All Ioan wanted was to be happy.

Passing the TV, he switched it on and eventually found a film that wasn't Christmas related before heading to the kitchen. It was nearing lunch, so he made himself a sandwich, grabbed a hot drink and settled on the sofa. He had no plans for the rest of the day except to veg out in front of the TV. He didn't often allow himself to do nothing on his days off, but he wasn't in the mood for anything else.

As he sat watching the film, his thoughts turned, yet again, to Colton. There was something about him that called to Ioan. Maybe it was the way he treated his mother or his good manners. Ioan didn't know, but something made him take notice.

After the fiasco with Axel, Ioan intended never to do the long-distance thing again. As he found out, who knew what the other person was doing when they were far away from their partner. Each person only knew what the other person told them. It took a lot of trust, which he'd thought he had in Axel, only to be told through a friend that Axel was sleeping around on him. Long distance was a thing of the past for Ioan. He just wished his brain would catch up to the fact.

The following morning, Ioan woke early. He'd not been inclined to head into work before his shift started at noon, but his brain thought otherwise. His dreams had been filled with Colton and several times, he had woken, sweating, with his cock as hard as steel. Try as he might, he hadn't been able to resist wrapping his hand around his dick and stroking himself to completion.

It would be Colton's last day—or partial day—with Rose, and as much as Ioan knew Colton didn't need him, Ioan couldn't help but feel like he might be able to make the separation a little easier for Colton.

He showered and dressed before bundling himself up for the bike ride to work. The temperature had dropped even more overnight, and Ioan hoped there was no snow in the forecast. He parked his bike at the nursing home, knowing he wouldn't be able to carry the drinks safely on the bike, then headed down the street to the bakery. As he entered the shop, he inhaled deeply and smiled. Just the scent of the bakery had his spirits lifting.

"Hey, Ioan! What can I get you?"

"Morning, Audrey. Could I have two pain au chocolat and a mocha and a spiced pumpkin latte, please?"

"Of course, you can." She entered the items into the register then passed the printout to Theo, the new baker, who also worked as a barista. "Is your American friend still here?"

"Oh, he's not my friend. He's..." Ioan paused, not knowing how to explain. "I suppose he is a friend," he muttered to himself. "Yes, he's still here, but he leaves for New York today. I'm just grabbing him a drink for the journey."

"Oh, that's nice of you. I can't imagine how long that trip must be."

"Yeah. A long way." He laughed.

He moved out of the way when another customer came in and waited for the order to be finished. He thanked Theo when he passed it over, and Ioan headed out the door with a wave. As cold as it was, he didn't want to rush and spill any of the drinks, so he walked slowly to the nursing home. When he entered the heated foyer, he blew out a breath.

"What's got you here so early?" Laura came out from behind the desk.

"Um..." He hadn't thought about what he'd be using as an excuse to explain his being there.

Laura's eyes twinkled. "He's still in with Rose, but he said he's leaving in..." she checked her watch, "twenty minutes. You made it just in time." She winked and carried on walking.

"I'm not...I didn't..."

Her chuckle floated back as she waved a hand above her head without turning around.

Ioan stared at the drinks and swallowed. The only person he apparently was kidding was himself. He sighed and shook his head. Regardless of his feelings, it wasn't going to happen.

Refusing to interrupt their final moments, Ioan

waited by reception, drinking his mocha and eating his breakfast until Colton arrived. Ioan's heart hammered in his chest the closer he came.

"Morning."

Colton's voice was gravelly and hoarse, and his eyes a little red as if he'd been crying. Ioan's heart went out to him. As much as he knew how it felt to leave his dad, at least he was only a couple of *hundred* miles away, not several thousand miles.

"Morning," Ioan whispered. "You okay?"

Colton huffed and shook his head. "Not really." He sniffed and exhaled.

"It's not much, but I have something for you." Ioan's hand trembled as he indicated the drink and food. "I thought you might want something before you go."

Colton stared at the items, his lips rolling inwards. "Thank you," he croaked.

"Tell you what. Why don't you eat and drink these here, then I'll give you a ride back to your hotel? It saves you walking in this freezing weather." He huffed. "I know it will be colder on the bike, but it would be for a smaller amount of time."

"Are you sure?"

Ioan nodded. "My shift doesn't start yet, so I have time."

"Thank you."

Ioan wanted to give Colton the experience of being on a bike again, and he couldn't resist having Colton wrap his arms around him one more time before he left. Selfish, yes, but unavoidable.

When Ioan swung his leg over his bike and steadied it

while Colton climbed on, his heart was pounding. He hoped Colton wouldn't be able to feel it through his clothes. The trip took less than fifteen minutes with the traffic, but it went by far too fast for Ioan's liking. He settled the bike at the kerb and waited for Colton to disembark before he followed. He pulled his helmet off, resting it on his seat as he attached the spare Colton had worn back into its place.

"I hope you have a good journey home. Even if it will be a long one." Ioan smiled.

Colton stared at him for a moment, then moved in and wrapped his arms around Ioan. Ioan could do nothing more than return the embrace. He closed his eyes as he inhaled Colton's scent, then forced himself to pull back.

"Thank you for everything, Ioan."

Colton leaned forward and pressed a kiss to Ioan's cheek, then turned and walked away.

Ioan blew out a breath, tears threatening to fall.

CHAPTER FIVE

COLTON

2018

The downside to expanding his stock was that Colton had less space on his stall unless he wanted to pay out for a larger one, which defeated the object of increasing his profit margin—at least for the moment. Having taken Zak's advice last year, he included custom wooden picture frames, small and large; mirrors, having carved the wooden frame; step stools, for adults and children; and little wooden chairs. He would've loved to be able to create some larger pieces, but he didn't have the space in his apartment to be sawing and moving large items of finished furniture up and down the stairs. His neighbours would probably kill him.

The upside was that his income had increased. If he sold the stock he had by the end of his season, he would seriously consider booking a larger space next year.

Thanksgiving hadn't been as quiet as usual. Dani had

invited him to her parents' house, and the number of people there had rivalled Uncle Brian's. In fact, it had probably been more. After they'd eaten all they could manage, they'd practically waddled to meet up with Jimmy. Colton had been more than happy to head home and collapse on his sofa, not moving until it was time for bed. He had ignored dinner time because he was still full from earlier in the day.

The following morning had been back to the grind, and it had been crazy busy, as was to be expected now they were in the run up to Christmas.

Christmas. Every time he thought of the word, he thought about Ioan. It had been eleven months since he'd seen him, but he was still never far away from Colton's thoughts. Every time, he kicked himself about their parting kiss. Colton had wanted nothing more than to grab Ioan and kiss the ever-loving fuck out of him, but he'd refrained. At the time, he'd thought it was a good idea, but now, he realised he should've done it. Even if it ended with a slap.

Colton had considered ringing the nursing home to speak to him, but the further away Christmas had become, the harder it was until too much time had passed. He still spoke to his mother once a week, but he refused to ask about Ioan.

"Do you have these in different coloured wood?"

Colton transferred his attention from his thoughts to the lady stood in front of him. "At the moment, the frames are only available in this grain and stain. I will be bringing in some newer colours early next year."

The lady thanked him and carried on looking. Colton

checked what stock he could put out and turned to the boxes behind him.

"These frames are amazing."

The English accent didn't throw him as Colton regularly heard all different accents. No, what threw him was that he recognised the voice. He spun around, gaze going directly to the man whose head was covered by a burgundy beanie and whose body was encased in a large jacket complete with burgundy scarf. His head was bent over the stall as his leather-gloved fingers traced some of the items. Regardless of not being able to see his face, he knew who it was.

"Ioan?" he croaked.

The man lifted his head, eyes wide. "Colton! I knew you lived in New York, but I never believed I'd see you in a place this big!"

"You should've called to say you were coming. I could've shown you around."

"Oh…I didn't think…"

Two guys came up to the stall, one of which pulled Ioan's beanie further down his face, ending his and Colton's staring contest.

"Push off, Nick," Ioan grumbled as he righted his hat.

"What've you found?" the other guy said.

"Um…this is Colton, Rose's son. Colton, this is Kyle and Nick."

"Rose? From the nursing home?"

Ioan nodded, gaze still lingering on Colton. Colton held out his hand to the two guys, not sure what relationship they had with Ioan but not wanting to be an ass.

"Nice to meet you…finally," the one called Nick said.

Ioan elbowed him, which Nick ignored. They stood in silence for a moment before Colton got his bearings again. He rounded the front of the stall and pulled Ioan into a hug. It was probably more than he should have done, but he couldn't resist.

"It's nice to see you again," he whispered in Ioan's ear.

Ioan's arms tightened briefly, then he let go. "You, too."

"Would you…like to grab for a drink with me after I finish today?" Colton asked, swallowing hard.

"Um…yeah. I'd like that."

Colton beamed. "Great. I finish at eight. Is that too late?"

Ioan shook his head. "That'll be fine."

"Okay. If you come back here, we can walk to the bar?"

Ioan smiled. "Sure."

Colton couldn't look away from the brandy-coloured orbs except to take in the flushed skin and reddened nose. Unable to help himself, he lifted his head and kissed Ioan's cheek for a second longer than needed.

"See you later."

With his lip in between his teeth, Ioan waved and spun, joining the two guys who were waiting a few steps away. Colton hadn't even realised they had moved. He watched as Ioan got swallowed up by the crowd, then returned behind the stall.

"Who was *that*?" Dani asked as she entered the back of the stall.

"Who?"

"You know who! That beautiful, flushed guy that you just kissed."

"I didn't kiss him!" Colton said.

"Okay, you kissed his cheek. It's still kissing."

Colton sighed. "He's Mom's caregiver."

"From England?" Her eyebrows rose at Colton's nod. "What are the chances?" She squinted at Colton. "Is he who you've been mooning over?"

"I haven't been mooning over anyone!" Colton opened a box to grab a few things he could fill the stall with. It had nothing to do with avoiding Dani's gaze.

"If you say so."

"I'm not!"

Dani raised her palms in a calming gesture. "Okay! Fine." She huffed. "What do you need help with?" Colton had messaged Dani asking for her help around half an hour ago.

"I need to grab something to eat and use the bathroom."

"Sure. I'll keep an eye on everything."

Colton frowned at her tone, not liking the way she said *everything*, but he ignored it. "I'll be back as soon as I can."

Dani waved him away as she dealt with a customer. He waded his way into the throng of people and headed to where he knew the toilets were. Once he had finished, he checked out some of the food stalls, deciding to go with a burger and a few small snacks to keep him going for the next three hours.

When he returned, and while he ate, Dani explained

what had been sold. "So, are you meeting up with that guy while he's here?"

Colton didn't want to answer but knew she would continue to bug him if he didn't. "Yes, after I finish tonight."

"Exciting!" Dani grinned.

"We're just friends, Dani."

"Uh-huh. And I'm the Queen of England." Dani rolled her eyes. "You should introduce him to us."

"No way."

"Oh, come on, Colton! Why not? It looked like he had two yummy friends." Dani grinned.

Colton sighed. "I'll ask Ioan if they want to meet up tomorrow for a drink with us. It's not my fault if he says no."

"That's all I ask." Dani fluttered her eyelashes at him.

"No guarantees."

Colton returned his attention to his burger. He wondered how long Ioan had been in New York already and when he was leaving for home. To think he may have missed out on several days with him hurt, but at least he was seeing him that night. He couldn't wait.

Colton was nervous as he packed away his stuff. As the clock ticked closer to eight o'clock, he couldn't stop himself from fidgeting and pacing behind the stall. He had no idea if Ioan was even going to show up. If he did,

Colton planned to take him to the bar he usually went to with Dani and Jimmy when he did this particular market.

"Hey."

Colton glanced up at Ioan, bundled up in his winter gear as he had been earlier. His gaze flicked to the side, seeing Ioan's two friends a few steps away. His heart dropped as he realised they would have chaperones. Not that they were going to do anything they shouldn't.

"Hi. Are you ready to go?" Colton said with a smile.

"Yes." Ioan turned to his friends. "I'll see you later."

Nick nodded. "Message me when you're ready to come back, and I'll come and fetch you."

"I'll bring him back. I...mean if that's alright?" He gazed at Ioan, who was staring at him.

Without glancing away from Colton, Ioan said, "I'll be fine with Colton, Nick. But I'll message you when we leave for the hotel."

Their gazes didn't leave each other as Colton exited from the back of the stall. "It's not far." He indicated the direction they needed to walk, and they started strolling side by side. The market had closed now, and there were only a few people lingering around. Despite the cold weather, Colton's body was warm and not just because of the clothes. He still berated himself for not kissing Ioan when he left Cambridge last year, but he knew there was too much time between interactions for him to go straight for it now. For all he knew, Ioan was in a relationship. He didn't even know if Ioan was gay, in all honesty, although he thought he was.

The bar was on the opposite side of the road to the market, all lit up festively but not particularly busy, thankfully. It meant they were more likely to get a seat. Colton led Ioan to a table near the bar but off to the side so they'd have a bit of privacy.

"What would you like to drink?" Colton asked.

"A beer would be good. I'm not fussed what kind." Ioan stripped off his gloves, hat, scarf and coat and piled them onto the seat next to him before resting his elbows on the table.

"Sure. I'll be back in a minute." Colton shucked his coat and draped it on the back of his chair before heading for the bar.

Colton was glad for the reprieve for a moment. While he wanted to spend more time with Ioan, he wasn't sure what to say. He certainly wasn't going to divulge his feelings and thoughts when they'd only just met up again. Grabbing two beers, he returned to their table, studying Ioan as he approached. Ioan was surveying the room, and he occasionally smiled as he saw something he obviously liked.

"Here you go." Colton set the beer in front of Ioan, then sat across from him once more. He stared at his beer, swiping his fingers through the condensation.

"Everything here seems so much bigger," Ioan said in a soft voice, eyes wide in what appeared to be wonder.

Colton tried to look around as if he'd never seen it before, but he knew what Ioan meant. "It is, basically." He chuckled. "Everything is three times as big as Cambridge for sure."

"It's strange. I feel so small." Ioan laughed.

Smiling, Colton leaned forward, closing a little of the distance. "What made you decide to visit New York?" He wished Ioan's answer would say *him*, but he realised that was too much to ask for.

"Kyle and I had always wanted to visit, but we'd never been able to afford it before. We've both been saving for a few years to be able to come. It's only a long weekend, but…" Ioan trailed off and shrugged.

Colton swallowed, not wanting to ask the next question but needing to. "When do you leave?"

Ioan licked his lips and stared at the table. "Tomorrow."

Colton held his breath and closed his eyes. He'd thought they'd get at least a couple of days before Ioan had to leave, not one night. "Best make the most of your company then." He forced a smile. "My friends won't be happy." At Ioan's blank look, he added, "They wanted to meet you."

Ioan's cheeks darkened. "How's the stall going?" Ioan took a sip of his beer, his tongue tracing his lips afterwards.

It was all Colton could do to concentrate. "Um…it's going well. Better than last year. I took the advice of someone I met in Cambridge, and it seems to have worked."

"That's great."

They swapped news about their jobs, Ioan catching him up on some of the staff and residents news. By the time Ioan was steadily yawning, it was past eleven.

"What time is your flight tomorrow?"

"Nine." Ioan yawned again. "Sorry. I've not really recovered from the jet lag." He snorted.

"Yeah, it's not easy when it's only a few days." Colton

didn't want to but said, "Let's get you back to your hotel."

They bundled themselves up again after Ioan sent a message to Nick telling them they were on their way, then exited the bar into the freezing night air.

"Shit, this is cold." Ioan pulled his scarf further up his face, shielding it from the frigid temperature.

"This is nothing. Be grateful you've come now and not in a month or so."

"Oh, so now I know why you come to the UK for Christmas. It's to get away from the cold," Ioan joked.

When Ioan shivered again, Colton didn't resist and pulled Ioan's arm through his, tucking him close. Ioan didn't object.

"We'll get a cab. It'll be warmer."

"No, I'm good. It's not that far away."

"Which hotel did you choose?"

"Washington Square Hotel."

"Nice. Let's get going; otherwise, you'll turn into a popsicle."

They didn't speak much apart from Colton pointing out certain landmarks he was sure Ioan knew about already. As much as he wanted to keep walking forever, he knew Ioan was freezing, so he moved as quickly as Ioan could manage.

Entering the large foyer of the hotel, they both sighed when the heat began to warm them. Colton led Ioan over to the elevators but stopped before pressing the button.

"I'll leave you here. Thank you for coming for a drink with me."

"Thank you for inviting me. I'll see you in a few weeks?"

The words were asked as a question, and he nodded. Colton's gaze roamed Ioan's face, but he still didn't have the courage to try for what he wanted. He leaned in and kissed Ioan's cheek once more, closing his eyes when Ioan gripped the front of his coat. Pulling away slowly, he whispered, "Goodnight," then walked backwards a few steps before turning and walking away.

It was so much harder than last time.

CHAPTER SIX

IOAN

Although Ioan needed to be up early, he couldn't sleep. His mind still lingered in the foyer of the hotel where Colton kissed his cheek. Ioan had felt it all the way to his toes and had to hold onto Colton; otherwise, he would have been on the floor. Lifting his hand, he rested it against his cheek as if he could still feel it. Ioan had no doubt that Colton liked men; he might like women as well, but it wasn't up to Ioan to put a label on him. There was no way Colton could've kissed him like that—twice—and not have some interest in Ioan.

An uncomfortable feeling went through him, and he flipped over to his other side. Light permeated through the thick curtains…New York alive and bustling despite the late hour. The differences in their worlds had become apparent when they were sitting in the bar. Ioan knew Colton didn't live 'large,' so to speak, but the city he lived in was unlike any Ioan could've imagined. There was no way he could live in such a big place, and he knew nothing could persuade Colton to move to Cambridge— his mother was there, and that didn't seem to be a big enough incentive.

Ioan groaned into his pillow. He had no idea why he was even entertaining the idea of them being together. It wouldn't happen. They were too far apart.

His alarm blared through the silence, making him jump. He must've slept some, but his head was pounding. Dismissing the alarm, he sat up and rubbed his hands over his face and through his hair. He was going to have to sleep on the plane; there was nothing else for it.

Luckily, he had packed all his things apart from his toiletries and the clothes he was wearing home. He climbed into the shower and made the water as cool as he could stand, hoping it would wake him up. When he'd finished packing his final items, he checked around the room once more to see if he'd forgotten anything.

A knock sounded. Ioan opened the door to Nick and Kyle.

"You ready?"

"Yep." Ioan grabbed his suitcase and backpack and followed the two men down the corridor to the lifts. "Are we grabbing breakfast here or at the airport?"

"The airport. It will make the wait a little easier, I think," Kyle replied.

Ioan nodded. They had to wait two hours at the airport before boarding their flight home. He'd probably buy another book before they boarded, having finished the one he'd bought in England for the flight to New York.

The taxi waited outside the hotel for them once they

had finished returning their keys to reception. The hour-long journey to JFK flew by in silence. At least, Ioan was silent. Kyle and Nick carried on a conversation, but Ioan had no idea what it was about. His thoughts were still on Colton.

When they finally arrived at the airport, Ioan was exhausted. He followed behind Kyle and Nick, not really paying attention to where he was going.

"Ioan!"

He scanned the airport, recognising the voice. Colton strode towards him, and Ioan's heart leapt.

"Hey, sorry. I didn't know if I'd catch you or not." Colton was out of breath. "Here." He held out a paper bag, and Ioan took it with a frown.

"What…?"

"You brought me a latte before I left last year, so I thought I'd return the favour and get you a pastry." Colton grinned.

Ioan shook his head. "What are you doing here?"

"I just came to say goodbye and bring you a drink." Colton pushed his hands into his coat pocket and stared at the floor.

"Thank you." Ioan wished they could be more than friends. He would love nothing more than to wrap his arms around Colton and never let go, but he kept reminding himself about the distance, and he didn't really know Colton all that well.

"Well, I'll let you get going."

Colton stepped forward, and Ioan knew he was going to kiss his cheek again. The closer he came, the harder Ioan's heart pumped. As Colton's lips brushed against his cheek, Ioan was unable to stop himself from turning his head so that their lips met instead. Colton pulled back, and their eyes met. Something must have shown in his face because Colton cupped his cheek and closed the distance again.

Their mouths pressed together, and Ioan's eyes fluttered shut. He gripped the front of Colton's coat as Colton's tongue teased along Ioan's lips. Ioan opened with a gasp, and their tongues slid against each other.

Colton pulled away, resting their foreheads together, sharing the same air. Colton lifted his head, pressed a kiss to Ioan's forehead and let go. "Safe journey home."

Ioan studied Colton's expression, seeing lines bracketing his mouth and eyes. He knew at that moment, they shouldn't have done that.

"I'll see you soon." Colton turned and walked away, and Ioan watched as he was swallowed up by the crowd.

"You okay?" Kyle's voice broke his concentration, and Ioan glanced at him.

"No."

Kyle nodded. "Come on. I sent Nick on to find a place to eat. I didn't think you'd want another witness."

Ioan didn't say anything, just turned his attention to getting through security and out to the departures area, where they headed for the restaurant Nick had messaged Kyle about.

"What's up with you?" Nick asked after they ordered.

"Nothing."

"You've been quiet since we knocked on your door this morning. Did something happen last night?"

No, something happened a few minutes ago. "No. We

had a few drinks, then he walked me back to the hotel. That's it." Ioan refused to mention the kiss because Nick would read more into it than they should.

"Hmm."

Ioan tried to keep up with the conversation, but he struggled. "I'm going to see if I can find a book. I'll meet you at the gate in a bit?"

"Sure. Ring us if you need anything."

Ioan nodded at Kyle, grabbed his backpack and wandered towards the shops. The kiss he and Colton had shared had been short but sweet, and Ioan wanted more. He had no idea how he was going to get through the next few weeks before he saw Colton again. And when he did see him, what the hell was he going to say and do? How was he going to face Rose?

Trailing around a few shops, he checked out their bookshelves, not finding anything that piqued his interest. Gay romance was not something widely available at most bookstores, so he'd have to settle for some non-fiction probably. Although he could also just forget about it and sleep instead. After drifting through the shops for a little longer, he gave up and headed to his gate. They still had just under an hour before the flight would be called, but Ioan couldn't be bothered to search any longer.

Kyle and Nick were sat in front of the huge windows, concentrating on their phones. Ioan dropped beside Kyle and rested his head against the cold glass, closing his eyes.

"Did you find something?" Nick asked.

"Nope. Choices were shit."

"You need to get yourself an e-reader or at least something for your phone. One of these days, you'll cave."

Kyle snorted. "I don't doubt it. He'll have no choice soon. Books are not going to be available much longer, I'm sure."

Ioan chuckled. "Well, until they are no longer sold, I will stick with them. They are so much better."

"How would you know?" Kyle bumped his shoulder.

"I have read a book through my phone before. It just doesn't have the same feel to it as a physical book."

"Whatever. You'll give in soon."

Ioan didn't reply, content to drift in-between awake and asleep until their flight was called. Once they boarded and the plane was taxiing to the runway, Ioan stared out of the window, looking at the view, knowing what he was leaving behind. As the plane lifted into the air, Ioan watched the buildings grow smaller and smaller, wishing he could find a way for their relationship to work but knowing it was a lost cause. There was no way they could afford to fly back and forth between Cambridge and New York regularly, and in between, not seeing each other would be painful.

Ioan rested his head against the wall of the plane, gaze still on the view outside, which was mostly clouds. When the ground was too far, Ioan closed his eyes, breathing deeply against the pain. He'd only met the guy a few times. Why did Colton have such an effect on him?

The following few days were excruciatingly long. The day after their flight he tried to sleep but kept being distracted by how quiet everything was, and the day after that, he'd been back at work. He'd been put in charge of organising the Christmas festivities again. Not that he minded, but he would've preferred to take a backseat this time.

Everyone had been so excited to talk to him about New York and see the photos he'd taken. He hoped they would eventually forget about it because whenever his thoughts drifted in that direction, the only thing he could see was Colton as he walked away from him at the airport.

Only Laura had asked if he'd seen Colton; the others probably hadn't thought of the connection. He'd admitted to Laura that he had seen Colton briefly and that he'd confirmed the date he was arriving. She'd not asked any other questions, although he had received a strange look which he couldn't decipher.

"Good morning, Rose."

Ioan entered her room, starting the morning routine just as Rose liked it. She was very set in her ways, which Ioan loved because he knew what each day would be like, except when she was having a bad day.

"Good morning, Ioan." He waited. "How long until Colton is here?"

Ioan couldn't help except smile, despite the topic. He

went over to her calendar. He had circled the date Colton had told him he would be visiting, which he knew was the day after he arrived in the UK. Even though Rose could see it on her calendar, she still asked the question. "You have seventeen days, Rose. Not long at all."

"A year is a long time to go without seeing my son." She sighed as she sat back in her chair.

"It is, but just think of how much you'll have to talk about."

"I wonder if he's found a partner yet. I always worry that he's all on his own over there. I know he has his friends, but it's not the same. I want him to find someone to share his life with."

Ioan swallowed hard at her words. He had no idea what he could say, especially when his thoughts went straight to him jumping up and down shouting "Pick me!"

"I'm sure he will find someone when he least expects it."

Ioan had.

"Yes, but I would've loved to see it for myself."

"You will. When he finds someone, I'm sure you'll be the first to know."

He worked through the remainder of his shift, trying to ignore images of Colton with someone else. Dropping his keys onto the table in the hallway of his house, he kicked off his shoes before taking off his coat and hanging it up. The kitchen called his name, and although he was starving, he had no energy to cook. Heading straight for the drawer that held the takeaway menus, he dialled, rattled off his order then threw himself on the sofa to wait.

Seventeen days, he'd told Rose. He had seventeen days to figure out how he was going to face Colton without dropping to his knees and begging him to stay in the UK. Seventeen days in which to figure out how to get rid of how he felt about the guy. Seventeen days to stop his heart from breaking.

He needed seventeen years, not seventeen *days*.

Ioan tried to fill his days off as much as he could with things that needed to be done. He had plans to visit his dad between Christmas and New Year and managed to pick up some gifts ready to take with him. For Kyle, he'd found a set of wireless headphones, which he thought would be good because Kyle always complained that the ones he had didn't work properly when he was at the gym. As for Nick, he would be receiving a gaming gift card, the perfect gift for a hardcore gamer.

His shifts at the nursing home were good for the most part. The only time he struggled was when he had to see Rose. As much as he loved the woman, he could see Colton in her appearance. It hurt every single time.

As the time for Colton's arrival drew nearer, Ioan found himself unable to concentrate. They had not communicated in any way since Ioan had left New York, although he knew Colton rang his mother every week as usual. Ioan needed a distraction, so he arranged to meet up with Kyle at a bar for a few drinks.

"What *is* up with you?"

Kyle knew about the kiss with Colton, having witnessed it, but he knew nothing else. Ioan hadn't planned to blurt everything out, but as soon as he started, he couldn't stop.

"And he arrives in three days." Ioan drained his beer after unloading on Kyle.

"Okay. So, what's the problem?"

"What's the problem?" Ioan stared at him, mouth open. "I just told you what the problem is. He's coming here in three days."

"You like him. He seems to like you. You haven't spoken, but I don't think three weeks is going to change things much. Just act like you normally would when you see him. Or better yet, grab him and kiss him."

Ioan rested his head in his palms, wishing he had never said anything to Kyle.

"You can't put him in the same bowl as Axel. Axel was an asshole. Colton doesn't appear to be."

"But that's the thing. How do I know? I hardly know anything about him. He lives three thousand miles away. And we'd only see each other once a year. How is that going to be any kind of relationship?"

"You just said it yourself. You hardly know anything about him. So maybe you need to get to know him. Invite him out while he's here, see what happens. Stop borrowing trouble."

"Okay, so what if things go well? Then what? Do I wait for him every year? Do I hold my breath every time the phone rings, hoping he's not ringing to break up with me? How does a relationship work from so far away? I couldn't manage it with Axel. How the hell can I manage it from here to New York?"

And that was the problem.

CHAPTER SEVEN

COLTON

Three weeks had felt like a hell of a long time despite how busy Colton had been. He'd been overrun with business on his stall and had sold almost everything he had hoped to. It meant, the following year, he could expand a little further. Maybe he'd seek out Zak while he was in Cambridge. It would be nice to see how Zak's business was growing, too.

When he finally set his suitcases down and dropped onto the bed, he was exhausted. If he had the energy, he would go find Ioan and explain how he felt, and in a perfect world, everything would work out between them, but he knew that was too easy. He had purposefully not called him because he didn't want to seem pushy, but now he was here, Colton wondered if it might have been the wrong choice, just like it had been the year before. Anything could happen in three weeks.

The first obstacle they would have to figure out was the distance. Colton's life was in New York, and Ioan's was in Cambridge. He had no idea how it would work, and maybe he was selfish for trying to start something with Ioan when he knew they would have problems with the mileage. Neither would be able to afford to see each other more than once a year, twice if they were really lucky. It was a difficult situation, and one he couldn't figure out alone.

He yawned and resolved himself to having to wait for answers. Closing his eyes for a moment, he sighed, wishing he could wave a magic wand and have everything turn out perfect.

He woke up later to a completely dark room, trying to figure out where he was. When his brain caught up, he sat upright and checked his watch. 4 a.m. He needed to try and sleep some more before the morning—later morning. Undressing in the dark, he stripped to his boxers and slid under the covers. Excitement raced through him when he thought about seeing both his mother and Ioan.

"Stop it and go to sleep," he muttered to himself. Clearing his brain, he concentrated on his breathing, hoping to get himself back to sleep.

Morning came and woke Colton through the open curtains. He'd not thought to close them when he'd entered the previous evening. He blinked blearily, adjusting to the surprisingly bright sun glaring through the window.

Yawning, Colton flung the covers off and traipsed to the bathroom, relieving himself before hitting the shower. He'd hadn't even looked at the clock; therefore, he was surprised to find that it was almost ten o'clock. He was usually at the nursing home by now. Quickening his movements, he dressed and grabbed what he needed to take with him. Sliding his arms into his coat and jamming a hat on his head, he grabbed his keycard and phone.

Just under half an hour later, he entered the nursing home, butterflies swarming in his stomach.

"Colton! So nice to see you again." Laura stood as he came closer to the reception area.

"Hi, Laura. How are you?"

"I'm good, thanks. Rose has been looking forward to your visit, as always. And today is a wonderful day for it."

Colton let go of the tension he'd been unconsciously holding and smiled. "That's good to know. I'd better go and see her."

He wandered down the corridor, knowing he could bump into Ioan at any moment. He didn't, and he wasn't sure if he was happy or sad about that.

"Mom?"

"Colton!"

Colton moved across the floor and embraced his mother, feeling how small she was in his arms. He hated having to wait to see her, but there was no other choice. His mom wanted to live in the UK, and Colton wanted to live in New York. Each had their own lives to live.

"I'm so glad to see you, sweetheart. How have you been? How was the flight? Did you get enough sleep last night?"

"Woah! Hold on. One question at a time." Colton chuckled.

Rose smiled. "Sorry. I'm just so happy you're here."

"Me, too."

They sat in the comfortable armchairs that graced the room and spoke about what had happened since he last spoke to her. He explained his plans for the following year, and she beamed when she told him how proud she was of him. Laura came in when it was lunchtime, inviting them both to the dining hall. Colton frowned when Ioan hadn't made an appearance.

"Is Ioan still working here?" he asked his mother.

"Of course! It's his day off. He told me he'd be back tomorrow."

Colton had many emotions surging through him. Disappointment that he wouldn't get to see Ioan until tomorrow? Yes. Hurt that Ioan hadn't come to see him? Yes. Annoyance at himself for being annoyed at Ioan? Yes.

He tried to forget about Ioan for the rest of the day, but it was difficult when he left the nursing home while Rose slept. Getting his bearings again, he headed off down the street in search of the bakery Ioan had taken him to the last time he'd been there. After around ten minutes, he wondered if he was heading in the wrong direction when it finally came into view.

The scent of freshly baked goods made his stomach grumble as he entered. Eyeing the glass cabinet as he lined up in the queue, he decided to take a few things for the staff of the nursing home as well as him and his mother.

"Good afternoon. What can I get you?"

"Could I have ten cakes, a variety, please, then two eclairs and a pumpkin spiced latte if you have one."

The lady behind the counter narrowed her gaze at him for a moment before smiling. "You're Ioan's friend. From New York."

Colton's heart jumped at Ioan's name, but he nodded slowly, not really knowing if they were friends, but it was the easier answer. "Yeah. I'm sorry, but I don't remember you."

The woman waved her hand. "I didn't expect you to. There are too many English people here to remember everyone, but we don't get very many Americans. Your accent makes you stand out." She held out her hand. "Audrey."

"Colton. Nice to meet you."

She turned to the guy behind her, and he grabbed a couple of cardboard boxes, beginning to fill them with cakes. "What brings you back to Cambridge, Colton?"

"My mom is in the nursing home here. I come to visit every year."

"Oh, how wonderful. I bet that is an amazing treat for her." Audrey made his drink and passed it over, taking his proffered payment. "Are you here for the whole of Christmas and New Year?"

Colton shook his head. "I have to go back on the twenty-seventh."

"At least you get Christmas and Boxing Day with her."

Colton had never really understood Boxing Day, but he agreed with Audrey all the same. "It's her birthday the day after Christmas as well, so it works out perfectly."

"Well, I hope you have a wonderful visit with her. Make sure you come back again. You hear?"

"Yes, ma'am."

The guy behind the counter passed over the bagged cake boxes, and Colton waved goodbye as he left, the cold wind biting through his coat. He was surprised the woman had remembered him, although if they didn't get many American visitors, it was probably understandable. Ioan obviously went there a lot if he was so well-known. He smiled, then, remembering Ioan's comment about being bankrupt from visiting the bakery so often.

Colton sighed as he sipped his piping hot drink. He wished he didn't have to wait until the next day to see Ioan, but he didn't know anything about him to be able to track him down. If he tried to get information out of someone at the nursing home, they were either unlikely to tell him because it was confidential, or they were likely to ask too many questions. He would have to wait until he saw him.

He planned to go straight to bed that night but decided against it. He needed to keep his UK hours, or his time here would suck. Dragging himself into the shower, he cleaned up and dressed in his jeans and sweater. Tying his boots, he wondered whether he'd bump into Ioan, then pushed that thought aside. It would be nice to see Zak, though. If Colton didn't see him at the bar, he might message him to see if he wanted to meet up.

"I've made quite a few custom pieces now, and I redid all the woodwork in someone's hallway at the beginning of this year. Even if I say so myself, it turned out amazing, especially as I was rushing to get it done." Zak lifted the beer to his mouth.

"Why were you rushing?" Colton asked.

Zak chuckled. "Ashley was over her due date when I agreed to do the job. I told the client that if she went into labour, I'd have to finish it afterwards, which they were fine with. Luckily, I finished the day before her waters broke."

Colton whistled. "Nice timing. Congratulations on your new addition. What's your child's name?"

"Dane. He's already cheeky and has me wrapped around his finger. I can't imagine my life without him now, and it's only been eight months." Zak shook his head, a small smile playing on his lips.

"It's not just you that he has wrapped around his finger," Ethan piped up with a grin.

When Colton had entered Crush, he had immediately been accosted by Zak, greeted with a slap on the back as if they'd been friends for years. It had been a strange feeling, especially as they'd only met a couple of times a year ago, but it was also really nice. Zak re-introduced him to the friends he remembered meeting last year: Sean, Ethan and Max. They all had similar interests. Sean was an architect; Ethan was an architect student, still at university, though on his work experience; and Max was an interwior designer. Add in Zak as a woodworker, and they had a good overall knowledge of design.

"What do you expect, Ethan? Zak's the first of us to

have kids. It'll be your turn soon." Max smirked at Ethan's spluttering and winked in Colton's direction. If he hadn't been in Max's presence for the past two hours, Colton would've thought he was flirting with him, but Max flirted with *everyone*.

"Have you a significant other?" Sean asked him. Sean was the quietest of them all, mostly keeping his opinions to himself, except when Max needled him enough for Sean to respond.

His thoughts went to Ioan, but he couldn't, in good conscience, say yes when he didn't know where they stood. He cleared his throat. "No, not at the moment."

"Hmm." Max tilted his head and narrowed his eyes in Colton's direction. "But there is someone you like." A statement, not a question.

Colton felt his cheeks heat, and he studied the table.

"Sorry, ignore me. Although I will say, if you want to talk about it, we're here." Colton looked up as Max indicated the table's occupants. "You live miles away. It's not like we're going to bump into them."

Colton bit his lip. "You might." He had no idea why he had said that. These people were still almost strangers, and yet he had given them a key to unlocking his thoughts.

Max leaned his elbows on the table. "Oh, are we talking about an English knight?"

Colton snorted. "You could say that."

"Who do you know around here, other than the people at the nursing home and us? You didn't find them online, did you?" Max raised his eyebrows.

"No, not online."

Max sat back, still studying Colton as if he was a bug under a microscope. "Do we know anyone at the nursing home?" He glanced at the other three men, who shook their heads. "Guess your secret is safe, then. Who is it?"

"I think it's time I went home," Colton said with a smile.

"No way!"

"You can't leave us hanging!"

Max's and Ethan's voices joined together.

"Leave him be, you carnivores," Zak admonished.

Colton stood, leaning forward to shake hands with his friends—at least, he hoped he could call them friends now. Zak gave him a one-armed hug.

"Don't be a stranger now. Use the number I gave you last year." Zak grinned.

"I will. Thanks."

Colton waved a final goodbye and headed back to his room. He was strangely buzzed, but he knew he'd crash and burn as soon as he relaxed in bed.

It was lunchtime the following day before he was able to see Ioan. Colton hadn't sought him out that morning, not sure if he had started his shift yet, but he knew Ioan took care of his mother; therefore, sooner or later, he would have to visit her.

"Good morning, Rose." Ioan swept into the room, his gaze briefly stuttering on Colton before moving back to his mother. "Hi, Colton. Are you ready for your lunch, Rose?"

"Oh, am I. I'm hungry today. Must be all the fresh air I've had. Colton took me into the gardens earlier. All wrapped up, of course. But it was beautiful. The sky was…"

Colton's focus was on Ioan's movements. Apart from the initial acknowledgement, Colton received nothing else from Ioan. He frowned as hurt ran through him. Maybe Ioan regretted their kiss, and this was his way of avoiding the subject. Colton inspected his hands as Rose got ready for lunch.

"Are you coming, Colton?" his mother asked.

He glanced at Ioan briefly. "No, you go. I'm going to get a couple of things done, and I'll be back after your nap." He stood, heading closer to the door where Rose and Ioan were standing. Leaning down, he kissed Rose on the cheek. "Enjoy your lunch, Mom."

"I will. Take your time, sweetheart. Don't forget to do things you enjoy doing, too. You don't need to just see me."

Colton couldn't resist and pulled her in for a hug. "I know, but I love being with you. Cambridge can wait."

"Alright, so long as you're sure." She patted his cheek and exited the room.

Ioan hesitated, which gave Colton the chance he needed. "Would you meet me for a drink later?" Colton watched as Ioan's lip disappeared between his teeth, then Ioan nodded. "What time do you finish?"

"Six."

"Will you meet me at Crush?"

Ioan licked his lips. "Okay." He turned and walked away.

Colton smiled at the empty room, then left the nursing home, heading back to his hotel room. He had a few things he wanted to buy for Christmas presents, so he grabbed what he needed then headed out on foot. It wasn't far to the city centre.

Several hours later, Colton was sitting at a booth in Crush, far too early, despite knowing Ioan wouldn't be coming straight to him; no doubt he'd go home first. He hadn't been able to wait. When he'd said goodnight to his mother, he'd run back to the hotel, showered and changed, then was back before his hair had even dried. He regretted that decision with how cold the evening was. Now, he was waiting, watching the door every time it opened, and his heart raced then calmed more times than was probably healthy.

When Ioan finally entered, stopping inside the bar to remove his scarf and hat as his gaze roamed the room, Colton's heart was in his throat. How could he be so speechless without even talking to the guy?

Their gazes locked, and Colton felt everything slide into place.

CHAPTER EIGHT

IOAN

It hadn't been easy staying away from the nursing home on his day off. Ioan had wanted nothing more than to go and see Colton, but he didn't want to bring any attention to their…whatever they were. He didn't know where they stood, and it didn't settle well with him. When he'd finally seen him, Ioan had to keep swallowing the lump that had appeared in his throat. He'd wanted to grab Colton and never let him go, which had shaken him. Despite all the scenarios he'd thought of, that hadn't been one of them.

Now, as he walked towards Colton, the lump had reappeared. He tried to think of something to say before he arrived at the table, but he stood in front of Colton quicker than he realised.

"Hi," Colton said, standing when Ioan stopped.

"Hey." Ioan took the seat opposite Colton, even though he wanted to sit next to him, and dropped his outerwear on the seat beside him instead.

"I wasn't sure if you'd eaten, so I haven't ordered yet."

"I haven't, no. The food here is delicious."

Ioan grabbed two menus, handing one to Colton before focusing on the food choices. He already knew what he wanted, but he needed time to settle into Colton's company again. It was strange to think they had kissed, but they were still such strangers to each other. Ioan didn't often do that. He struggled with having casual hookups because he needed that emotional connection. That wasn't to say he didn't do it, just not often.

"Burger and fries sound good."

"Chips," Ioan automatically corrected, then bit his lip, peering at Colton over the top of the plastic to see Colton grinning. "Sorry."

"It's okay. I'm sure there are many more words we'll trip over during our conversation."

Ioan's shoulder released some more of their tension as the familiar camaraderie filled the air between them. "Probably." He smiled. "Same for me. Burger and chips." They placed their order, and Ioan asked, "How is the stall going?"

"Really well. I've hit my target this year, so that will make things easier next year. I'm hoping to expand a little more, too."

"That's great news. Congratulations."

"Thanks."

As their drinks were delivered and then their food, Ioan and Colton caught up on what had been happening in the three weeks since they'd seen each other, the background noise of conversation and laughter loud but not breaking their little bubble. It was almost as if they had never been apart as if New York had been yesterday. After all the agonising Ioan had been doing about what they would say to each other, he needn't have worried at all.

When their plates had been cleared, Colton leaned closer. "Are we going to ignore the elephant in the room?"

Colton's gaze bored into Ioan's, his eyes sparkling like quartz in the sunlight. Ioan licked his lips, and Colton groaned. Ioan hadn't realised his eyes had drifted to Colton's mouth until he lifted them to Colton's eyes once more, seeing the storm brewing.

"Do you want this?" Colton flicked a finger back and forth between them.

Ioan swallowed hard but nodded. "I don't know how it's going to work…"

"Let's not borrow trouble. Would you like to get out of here?"

Something snapped inside Ioan, and he nodded, standing from the seat and dragging his coat on.

Colton cupped his cheek as he stood in front of him. "My hotel, or your place?"

"Mine."

Without further conversation, they exited the bar into the freezing night. Colton grabbed Ioan's hand, linking their bare fingers together as they walked to Ioan's bike. Ioan held out the spare helmet, which Colton put on before pulling on his gloves, then he climbed on the back of the bike as soon as Ioan had it roaring to life. Even with the ability to converse through the helmets, they didn't speak a word, dismounting once they arrived at Ioan's house.

Ioan's heart was racing as he walked up the path to the front door. He hardly ever had men in his house, always preferring to go somewhere else, but there was something about Colton that he needed. That he wanted in his house. He wanted memories to tide him over.

As soon as the front door was locked behind them, Colton pressed Ioan into it. He cradled Ioan's face as he stared up at him, the few inches height difference never more apparent than then.

"I missed you."

Colton's words were the spark to the wood, and their lips clashed. Ioan gripped Colton's head, directing his movements, keeping their mouths fused as they fought to get closer. Ioan used his free hand to push at Colton's coat until it thudded to the floor. He removed his hands when Colton pushed at his own coat, their lips leaving then returning, depending on their actions.

Ioan started walking, slowly pushing Colton backwards as their lips and tongues explored. When Colton bumped into something, he spun Ioan around. Ioan moved a hand to the object, realising it was the sofa, then sat down on the arm of it. It made Colton's head higher than his. He pulled back, brushing his fingers over Colton's flushed cheek and across his lips.

They stared at each other as Ioan traced the contours of Colton's face, noticing the scar bisecting his right eyebrow.

"Ioan…"

Colton fused their lips together with such force, Ioan fell backwards onto the sofa, laughing as his legs lifted into the air.

"God, sorry."

Colton moved to help, but Ioan waved him off. He rolled off the sofa onto the floor, the burgundy carpet cushioning his knees. Before he could stand, Colton was surrounding him, arms caging him as his back and hips met flush with Ioan's. Ioan groaned as Colton's hard cock pressed against his ass, and Ioan pushed back, receiving an answering moan.

Colton mouthed at Ioan's neck as he rocked, increasing the friction. Ioan needed more. He dropped to his elbows, then twisted, rolling onto his back and spreading his legs on either side of Colton.

Although they were still fully dressed, Ioan felt naked. The look in Colton's pupil-blown eyes was enough to heighten his pleasure ten-fold. Colton's fingers slid under Ioan's jumper, lifting it higher and higher until he pulled it off, then Colton's lips were once again on his, sipping at his bottom lip.

"Colton…fuck!"

Ioan grappled with Colton's jumper, yanking it over his head and set to work undoing the buttons on his shirt. When there was enough space, he pulled that over Colton's head, too.

The heat of Colton's naked chest against his own had his hips lifting of their own accord, trying to find something to rub against. Colton's lips left his, nipping and licking his way down Ioan's neck and chest to his nipples. The hard points were straining for attention, which

Colton gave. With every nip, squeeze, lick and pull, Ioan groaned louder and longer.

Fingers fumbled with Ioan's jeans, and Ioan's nails raked through Colton's hair. With nothing to grab hold of, Ioan felt himself drifting. At least until Colton wrapped his hand around Ioan's dick. After the brief chill of the air on his overheated cock, the warmth from Colton's hand burned him. Ioan bucked, his head pressing into the floor as pleasure streamed through him.

"Fuck! Oh, god!"

Ioan became incoherent as Colton's mouth left his nubs and dropped immediately onto his shaft. He couldn't help but watch as his red, straining cock disappeared into Colton's mouth, appearing again shiny and wet. Seeing Colton like that was hot. Ioan felt Colton's tongue laving across his sensitive skin and flicking at the tip with every stroke. Ioan's hands clutched at Colton's bare back with nothing else to grab hold of.

Colton pulled off, breathing heavily. He kissed his way up Ioan's body until he reached his mouth. "Fuck me," he whispered against Ioan's lips.

Ioan's nostrils flared at the thought. He had thought Colton was a top. Not that it mattered to Ioan, who was vers.

Ioan pulled away, gasping. "Lube is upstairs." He pushed at Colton's shoulders, not wanting to move but wanting to be inside Colton more than anything.

They stumbled to the stairs, Ioan gripping the waistband of his jeans so he didn't fall.

"One day, we're fucking in front of that roaring fireplace," Colton said.

Ioan glanced at him and almost stumbled with the desire apparent on Colton's face. Yes, they were definitely doing that sooner rather than later.

Entering his room, he stepped to the side of the bed, retrieving lube and a condom and throwing them on the bed. As he removed his jeans and boxers, he watched a naked Colton crawl over the covers until he rolled onto his back and his head rested on the pillows. His ass was perfect. As was everything else. A brief flicker of anxiety flashed through him at the reminder that everything wasn't perfect, but Ioan brushed it aside, climbing over Colton.

"You sure?" Ioan didn't want Colton to regret this.

"Fuck, yes."

Leaning down, Ioan kissed Colton with everything he had in him. Their cocks slid together as their hips thrust, trying to race to the finish line. Ioan lifted off, wanting to be inside Colton before he came.

Unclicking the lid, he squirted some lube onto his fingers and shuffled back. He licked up the underside of Colton's cock, sucking on the head as his fingers prepared Colton's hole. Ioan's focus turned to Colton's face, watching his expression for any hint of discomfort. All he saw was pleasure, even when three fingers thrust in.

"Enough. Ioan, please!"

Ioan sucked hard as he dragged his mouth up and off Colton's shaft, licking his lips because the taste of Colton's precome aroused Ioan more.

He rolled the condom on, lubed it, then flipped Colton to his stomach and hitched him to his knees.

Bowing over Colton's back, he kissed a trail along his spine as his hand guided his cock towards Colton's hole.

Finding his goal, he gripped Colton's hip as he drove forward, seating himself slowly but steadily in Colton's ass. He paused, resuming his kisses to Colton's back until Colton's tension reduced and he began to move and whimper.

"All good?"

A moan was all he received which he took as proof. Ioan repeatedly withdrew and thrust, hands clutching at Colton's hips as he pounded into him, sweat beading on his skin.

"Fuck, Colt! Oh, hell! I'm not gonna last."

Colton dropped to his elbows, and Ioan assumed he was jerking off, which made Ioan even hotter.

"I'm almost…I'm…fuck! Ioan!"

Colton's ass clenched, strangling Ioan's cock. Ioan reached for Colton's shoulders, needing the extra resistance to his movements, and slammed into him, shouting his release even as he thrust deep and held himself there.

"Jesus, Ioan," Colton gasped.

Ioan said nothing, unable to string a sentence together after that. He stayed there for a few more seconds before holding the end of the condom and withdrawing, hissing at the sensitivity. Disposing of the condom in the bin by the bed, Ioan dropped onto his back and stared at the ceiling.

"I think you killed me."

Ioan snorted, rolling to his side and spooning Colton. "You want to stay?" he whispered.

Colton turned over so they were face to face. Skimming his fingers over Ioan's face just like Ioan had earlier, Colton said, "If that's okay?"

Ioan kissed him in answer.

Their days were spent on their usual routines: Colton with his mother and Ioan at work, but their nights were spent wrapped around and inside each other, as close as two people could get. Ioan loved every minute of it, but the shadow following them around tinged their union with sadness, at least for Ioan.

The morning Colton was departing for New York arrived bright but with a definite chill in the air. Ioan had requested to swap his shift at work so he could see Colton off at the airport. He was no longer trying to hide anything from the staff; there was no point. More than one had commented on their 'relationship' during the past week, but Ioan didn't have the heart to tell them it wouldn't happen.

After Colton had said goodbye to his mum, they grabbed his suitcases and headed to the airport in a taxi. The air was buzzing with unsaid words, but Ioan couldn't make himself say anything. He knew there was no way he would be able to deal with such a distance between them, and he cursed himself for putting them both through what he knew would be a difficult departure.

They swung by Sweet Tooth to grab a pumpkin

spiced latte for Colton's trip—it appeared to be a routine Ioan had unexpectedly started.

As they stood facing each other at the furthest point Ioan could go, he found he couldn't look at Colton. Instead, he studied his feet, scuffing them back and forth like a school child.

"Ioan…"

The crack in Colton's voice had Ioan closing his eyes against the pain tearing through his heart. As much as he hadn't wanted his heart to become involved, it seemed he'd had no say.

Arms wrapped around him, holding him tight, and he threaded his fingers through Colton's hair as Colton tucked his face into Ioan's neck.

"I can't do this, Colton."

He felt Colton stiffen before he pulled back, questions in his eyes that Ioan couldn't easily answer. "What?"

"I can't…I can't do long-distance." Ioan inhaled shakily as he tried to step back, stuffing his hands in his pocket.

Colton gripped his biceps. "What was all this, then? What was the point? If you knew this at the beginning, you should've told me!" Colton slid his hands up to Ioan's neck. "I'm…I…" Colton exhaled heavily, pulling a hand away to rub over his own mouth and jaw. "I don't know what to say," he whispered.

Ioan glanced at Colton, seeing lines deepening on his forehead and bracketing his mouth. The scar on his eyebrow more visible in his confusion.

"I'm sorry," Ioan croaked. A tear overflowed and dripped down his cheek, but he didn't wipe it away. If he removed his hands from his pockets, he didn't think he'd be able to stop himself from pulling Colton close and never letting him go. He knew himself, though. He knew he wouldn't be able to cope with the distance between them. He should have been strong enough to stop… whatever they were before it happened.

Colton shook his head. Sighing, he leaned forward, pressed a kiss to Ioan's cheek, whispered, "Goodbye, sweetheart," and walked away.

Ioan stared until Colton disappeared around the corner, then everything became blurry as his tears fell in a torrent.

CHAPTER NINE

COLTON

2019

As Thanksgiving came and went, Colton tamped down on his hope that he would see Ioan. He didn't even know why the thought had been circulating. He knew how expensive vacations were and that trips across the Atlantic were usually once in a lifetime for those who weren't well off. Colton wasn't rich, but he lived frugally so he could afford the flights every year. Ioan didn't need to fly here, especially when Colton would be back in Cambridge in three weeks. Besides, they hadn't spoken since the airport last year.

He wasn't bitter about that at all. Nope. Not at all.

Colton clenched his jaw and brushed the thought aside. Ioan had made his decision, and there was nothing Colton could do about it.

He dragged himself up the stairs to his apartment before stumbling inside. Exhausted didn't come close to how he was feeling; he hoped he wasn't getting a cold. That was the last thing he needed.

The notification sound on his phone had him retrieving it from his pocket. Jimmy.

Come on out with us.

Shaking his head, he ignored the message and set it on the table, opening the fridge for leftovers. Since he'd expanded his stock, he had been able to buy some proper food on occasion and made sure to cook enough to last him a few days.

With the food warming in the microwave, Colton leaned back against the wall and stared at the floor. He wished he'd tried to persuade Ioan to give them a chance. Since the moment Colton walked away, he'd regretted that he hadn't, but he'd seen the expression on Ioan's face and realised there'd be no point. He still wished he'd tried.

Every time he had spoken to his mom, he'd wanted to ask about the staff, hoping she'd mention Ioan, but he refrained. When his mother *had* spoken about Ioan, Colton had listened as if his life depended on whatever information she could provide. Once or twice, he'd heard someone in the background and strained to hear if it was him.

Dani and Jimmy were getting fed up with him. Whenever they went out, which wasn't nearly as much as it had been before Ioan, they pushed for him to find someone. They'd done that before, but now it was much less subtle. He'd had enough and so had taken to ignoring their messages and calls. It wouldn't last long. They'd be storming up the stairs sooner rather than later.

Plating his food, he sat in front of the TV and switched it on, not really caring what was on; he just needed the background noise.

When he put an empty fork in his mouth, he realised he'd finished his food, having tasted none of it. Colton closed his eyes, rested his head back and sighed. Maybe he did need to let Ioan go and have some fun. Problem was, he'd be right back where he started when he flew to Cambridge in a few weeks.

"Colton! Get your ass up right now!"

The shout followed by banging on his door had his pulse skyrocketing before he recognised Jimmy's voice. Apparently, much sooner than he thought.

Colton sighed again and put his plate in the sink before opening the door and staring at Jimmy and Dani. "What?"

"Get dressed."

Colton looked down himself. "I am dressed."

"Fine. Get *changed*." Dani pushed past him, stopping in the centre of the apartment with her hands on her hips.

"I'm not going out with you guys." Colton wandered over to the sofa and sank down, staring at the TV.

"The fuck you're not. You have been wallowing in this apartment for the last eleven months. Get the fuck over it. He's not here, he's not coming here, and I can almost guarantee he won't be waiting for your ass when you get there."

Colton gaped at Jimmy.

Jimmy blew out a breath. "Sorry, but it's the hard truth. Don't waste your life waiting for someone who doesn't want you."

Colton's shoulders dropped. He knew what Jimmy meant. Jimmy was still struggling with his feelings for Vanessa, and although Colton was still certain that Vanessa felt the same, neither were taking the chance. Maybe he or Dani needed to step in?

Dropping his head forward, Colton groaned. Like they were stepping in for *him*. Fucking hell.

"Fine. I'm not guaranteeing anything, but I'll come out. Only one drink. I'm exhausted, and I still have over three weeks left."

He trudged over to his bedroom and quickly changed his clothes, tidying himself up a bit. When he returned to the living room, Dani was pointing a finger at Jimmy's chest and talking quietly but stopped when she saw him.

"Alright, I'm ready."

A cab sat at the kerb, and they all piled in. Colton rested his elbow on the door and pinched at his lips repeatedly as he stared out of the window, watching the lights dance in and out of his vision as they sped past. He would love to show Ioan his home city. There were plenty of places that Ioan hadn't visited last year, he was sure. He'd probably just done the tourist things, but Colton knew some of the best places to visit, in his opinion.

Stomach fluttering, he wiped thoughts of Ioan away and remembered the message he'd received from Zak earlier that day. They had messaged back and forth over the past several months, both taking an interest in the other's business. This time though, Zak had contacted him asking if he wanted to hang out again when he was over in Cambridge, and Colton had readily agreed. He'd enjoyed meeting up with Zak and his friends the past two years, and it would be nice for him to do it again this time. Then, he wouldn't be bored in his hotel room every night.

The cab stopped, allowing them to climb out. Dani paid, and although Jimmy argued, he lost. As late as it was, the crowds were heavy, and they had to elbow their way through the masses to the bar. There was no way they'd be able to find a seat, so they stayed at the bar.

"Stop glaring at people." Dani nudged his shoulder, and he turned his glare to her, seeing her with a smirk.

"Shut up." He chuckled, then sobered. "I'm trying, Dani."

"I know, Colt. You need to let him go."

Colton had explained everything to Dani and Jimmy when he returned last year. He'd been a wreck for several days afterwards but managed to pick himself up when he needed to get back to work. He had a living to earn after all.

"It's not easy." He faked a smile and went back to staring around him. Then, he remembered Dani's date. "Oh, how did it go with your two guys the other day?"

Dani blushed. Her cheeks actually darkened to an adorable shade of pink. "It was good."

He waited for more, but when she said nothing, he prompted, "And?"

She nibbled her lip. "We're seeing each other again next week."

Colton's eyebrows rose. "Really? That's unlike you."

Dani downed some of her wine, then croaked, "I know." She gulped the rest of the wine, indicating she needed another from the bartender. She turned to Colton and shrugged. "I decided why not give it a try with a couple of guys I like. You never know."

Colton understood what she was trying to say. "I'm sure it'll work out great."

"Hey, I'm sorry to interrupt. I wondered if you were looking for someone tonight?" The guy smiled at Colton, so Colton gave him a once over. He was slightly shorter than Colton, slim and wearing skin-tight jeans and a t-shirt that gave a nice definition to his muscles. His blond hair was curling around his earlobes, his features soft yet strong. Any other time, Colton would have jumped at the chance.

"No, sorr—"

"Yes, he is!" Dani's voice overtook his, and Colton glared at her once more.

The guy squinted between the two of them before asking, "Are you his pimp or something?" He chuckled at his not-so-funny joke.

Dani narrowed her gaze on the guy. "No, he's just getting over a broken heart, so although he says he's not ready, he is."

The guy held out his hand. "Jordan. Nice to meet you."

Colton wrapped his hand around Jordan's. "Colton. You, too."

Jordan scooted into a space on the opposite side to Dani, and Colton twisted to see him. "So, Colton, what do you do?"

"I'm a woodworker. I have a stall where I sell the items I make."

"Nice! I'm a street performer. I work at some of the markets, so maybe I've seen you around."

Colton leaned his elbow on the bar as he drained some of his beer. "Maybe. What kind of street performer?"

"Oh, I'm a mime. Well, sometimes, I am. I also do the statue performances."

"That takes some patience. Do you enjoy it?"

"Yes, very much. You get to hear all kinds of things when you're stone still, and nobody thinks you can hear them."

"So many secrets…" Colton chuckled.

"Definitely. It's almost as if they think because I'm so still, my hearing is gone, too." Jordan drained his beer and set it on the bar.

"Can I get you another?"

Jordan nodded. "Thanks. Same again, please. So, what kind of things do you make?"

When Jordan had first approached him, Colton had come to the conclusion that Jordan was a rich kid who always got what he wanted. As their conversation progressed, he found the guy to be inquisitive, smart and witty, even if his jokes were a little off on occasion. They had moved closer and closer until there was barely any space between them without them actually touching, and for the first time in a long time, Colton had been interested in someone other than Ioan. He decided it wouldn't hurt to get to know Jordan a little more.

"Would you like to get out of here?" Jordan asked

into his ear. The breath on Colton's skin made him shiver involuntarily.

"Sure." Colton turned to let Dani know he was leaving and received a wink in return.

Jordan linked his fingers through Colton's and weaved through the crowd to the exit. Just before they left, they both put their coats on. The cold air whipped at Colton's face as they opened the door. Jordan twined their fingers together again, but instead of heading to a cab, he pushed Colton against the wall of the bar. When his lips pressed against Colton's, Jordan stepped into him, gripping Colton's coat.

Colton didn't push him away. He knew what had been silently agreed with the getting out of here question, so he held onto Jordan's hips and kissed him back. Jordan's tongue slid along Colton's lower lip. With a slight hesitation, he opened, hearing Jordan groan and press closer when Jordan's tongue touched his own. The kiss deepened, and Colton's hand came up to cup the back of Jordan's head as he ravaged the delicious mouth before him.

They pulled away, little puffs of steam escaping their mouths as they gasped for air. Jordan smiled at him, and Colton's stomach fell. Fuck.

"I'm sorry," Colton said.

Jordan frowned. "Why?"

Dropping his hands away from Jordan, Colton stared blankly behind Jordan. "I can't do this."

Jordan stepped back, cold air invading where he'd had been pressed against Colton, making Colton shiver. "You've just been doing this. What's the problem?"

"Ioan."

Jordan blinked. "That's not *my* name, so I can only assume Ioan is the problem." Jordan laughed, his expression hardening. "Thanks for nothing."

Colton watched Jordan storm off down the street and into a waiting cab. Sagging against the wall, Colton stared at the ground, his vision blurring. He felt numb where a few minutes earlier he'd felt warm. How could he hang onto something he knew was never going to happen?

Sniffing and wiping his face, he walked across to a cab and climbed in, giving his address. He pulled out his phone and messaged Dani and Jimmy in their group chat.

Heading home. Thanks for getting me out of the apartment.

Not waiting to see if they replied, he put it away and stared at the passing scenery. Dani was right. He needed to let go of Ioan, but he didn't know how he was going to do that, especially since he was seeing him again in three weeks. He wished someone would give him an answer.

The following morning, he pushed Jordan from his mind as he set to work. He'd managed to sell more of his stock and even had some custom items on order. They would be made just after New Year when he had time. He was slightly later leaving for Cambridge this year, due to what weekday on which Christmas fell, but he'd still be there for the full week as usual. He couldn't wait to see his mother. They hadn't been able to talk the previous weekend because his mom was having a bad day, so he'd spoken to the nurse for a short time to get an update and told her to email him if his mother wanted to speak to him before this weekend. He didn't make them call him as he knew costs could be expensive.

Yawning, he scratched at his beard, then scraped his fingernails along his scalp, trying to wake himself up a bit more. He needed to grab a coffee before the market opened, and he made a note to message Dani and Jimmy to see if one of them was in the area and could cover for him for a short time later in the day. They knew almost as much about his items as he did, and they were a godsend when he needed a ten-minute bathroom break. Most of the time, he had to rely on the stallholders around him to cover for him while he went, but he hated imposing on them.

After grabbing his coffee and a bagel, Colton returned to his stall just in time for the first wave of customers to come through. He chatted with each of them, asking about their needs and what they were looking for. He enjoyed the customer service side of things as much as making the items. Listening to people's stories and what they envision was enlightening, to say the least.

When the market came to a close, Colton was tired all over again but content with his business, nonetheless.

If it continued the way that it was, he'd be able to start saving some money for the future.

"Colton?"

Colton jerked his gaze up, staring into the brandy-coloured eyes he wished would be part of that future.

CHAPTER TEN

IOAN

Standing in front of Colton's stall was more nerve-wracking than the first time he'd done it. Of course, last time, he hadn't realised it belonged to Colton until later.

"Ioan?"

Ioan's eyes closed briefly against the sound of his name in Colton's accent. He'd missed it. When Laura had demanded he take time off and stop working himself to the bone, he could do nothing but accept it. She had given him a full two weeks, and he'd been wandering around his house like a lost puppy. Kyle and Nick had been no good. They kept telling him he needed to forget about Colton. Easier said than done.

"What are you doing here?" Colton came around to the front of the stall, and Ioan had to fight to keep his feet still.

"I don't know." His answer was soft, but so truthful, it hurt. "Laura gave me some time off. I had no idea what to do with myself until I found myself booking a flight." His throat felt thick, and his eyes burned.

Colton stepped forward and embraced Ioan tightly. Ioan tucked his head into Colton's neck and breathed him in. His hands gripped at the back of Colton's coat.

"I'm sorry, Colton. I'm so sorry," he whispered.

"Shh. It's okay. Everything's okay." Colton pulled back and cupped Ioan's cheek in his gloved hand. "Will you stay with me?"

Ioan's tears finally overflowed as he nodded. "Yes."

A smile crept across Colton's face until he was beaming, and Ioan felt his tension drain away. Colton's eyes flicked to Ioan's mouth when he licked his lips, and then he came closer. When their lips met, it was like an explosion. Ioan held on as tight as he could as Colton devoured him. He wanted to be as close to him as he could. This what he'd been missing all these months. This is what he needed. When they were together, they were stronger than ever.

Colton pulled away, breathing heavily. Ioan stared at him, dazed. "Let's go home."

Ioan helped Colton to finish securing his stall for the following day, then they walked hand in hand along the pavement.

"Where are all your things?" Colton asked.

"At my hotel. I wasn't sure what reception I'd get. I didn't want to assume you'd let me stay with you."

"We'll get a cab and grab your things. You can cancel your room and stay with me." He paused. "When do you leave?"

"On the eighth."

Colton smiled. "We have five days."

"Four, really. The flight is early. Sorry."

Colton smiled. "Don't be sorry. I didn't think I'd get to see you until Christmas. This is the best present ever. I've missed you."

"I've missed you, too."

They went straight for Ioan's things despite how late it was getting, extremely late for Ioan as he was still on UK time. Colton's argument was that it meant Ioan could sleep in the following morning without having to worry about anything.

When they finally arrived at Colton's apartment, Ioan was dead on his feet. Colton helped him get undressed, stealing kisses now and then, and tucked him into bed with Colton wrapped around him. The last thing he remembered was the heat from Colton's body seeping into his and warming his soul.

Ioan woke with a start, wondering where the hell he was. As he looked around the sparse bedroom, it took him a moment to remember. He smiled and checked the time on the clock. 10 a.m. Colton would already be at the market, and although Ioan would've liked to wake up with him, he was glad he'd had the chance to sleep.

He rolled to his back, arms outstretched. A crinkle of paper under his arm had him lifting it to his face.

Morning,

Sorry I didn't wake you. I wasn't sure how bad your jetlag would be, so I thought I'd better err on the side of caution and let you sleep. I've left a spare key for the apartment on the table. Feel free to use it as you need to. You don't have to come to the market if you want to go sightseeing. I should be back by around nine tonight. I'll make us some food once I'm home, or we can grab a some takeout. If you do want to come to the market, I'll be here. I'll stop rambling now and head out. I'll see you later.

C x

Ioan grinned and pressed the paper to his chest. There was nowhere he'd rather be than by Colton's side, even if he was busy working all day.

As he got out of bed, Ioan thought about what had made him come to New York. Kyle and Nick were fed up with him moping around, but Ioan couldn't do anything about it. He knew he'd made the right choice to leave things alone with Colton last year, but as this year had crept along, he'd been second-guessing himself. When he'd found himself looking at flights to New York, he knew he had to come, regardless of the outcome.

He had absolutely no idea how things were going to work out, but he had to try if nothing else.

The shower was small and had very low pressure, but at least the water was hot. Once he was sufficiently clean and dry, he dressed in his warmest clothes, knowing, from Colton's previous descriptions, that standing still for any length of time would be freezing. He grabbed the key from the table, slipping it into his wallet so he didn't lose it, wrapped himself up in his coat, hat, scarf and gloves, then exited the apartment.

Using his phone as GPS, he walked his way to the market. It took around half an hour, and then he was enfolded in the crowds seeking out wares from over one hundred stalls that Colton told him about. It was a sight to behold. Ioan took his time, looking at the different stalls as he wandered down to where Colton was situated.

Colton was serving a customer when he arrived, and Ioan stopped to watch him. The surety of his movements, the smile on his face and the sound of his laughter all worked together to make him approachable and honest. Ioan's heart hammered as he began to understand the enormity of what he'd just done. When he left for England again, he would have to believe Colton would be true to him until Colton returned to Cambridge. After booking the flight to New York, the only thing on Ioan's mind was seeing Colton; he hadn't thought further ahead than that. Now he was in the one position he had always said he would never be again.

"Ioan!" Colton's voice jerked him from his thoughts, and Ioan smiled as he walked over. "Come round the back."

Ioan shuffled through the gap, and as soon as he was behind the stall, he was embraced in a tight hug. "Nice to see you, too." He snorted.

"Excuse me? How much is this?"

From that moment on, they only had a few stolen minutes here and there, in between customers. They kissed, touched and cuddled as much as they could until someone else interrupted. He couldn't begrudge them, though. It was Colton's work, after all. Ioan had fetched them food and drink and had taken over the stall when Colton needed to use the bathroom—that had been unnerving. He couldn't answer many of their questions, but Colton had saved him by returning quickly.

By the time the market closed, Ioan was worn out.

"How do you do this every day?"

Colton chuckled. "I'm used to it. I've been doing this for…I can't remember how many years."

"Do you ever have breaks in between markets?"

"Of course. There isn't a market available every day, but I'd say, I work most of the year. Keeps the money rolling in."

"You enjoy this part of it as well, don't you?"

Colton glanced at him with a smile. "Yeah. Nothing beats having someone buy something you've created."

After the stall was packed up, they walked towards Colton's apartment. When they entered and removed their coats, Colton pinned him to the wall, taking Ioan's mouth in a bruising kiss. Ioan cupped the back of Colton's head as he twined his tongue around Colton's, the press of Colton's body against his increasing his need.

A knock on the door had them jumping apart.

"Hey, Geppetto! Open the door!"

"Fuck." Colton sighed, stroking a finger down Ioan's cheek. "Are you ready to meet my friends?"

Ioan's eyes widened as his pulse increased. "Now?"

Colton nodded, kissing Ioan briefly when another knock sounded.

"Colton!"

"Alright, alright." With an apologetic look, Colton

opened the door, and Ioan saw a tall—well, taller than Ioan's six feet—muscly guy with short spiky, blond hair and a woman with shoulder-length brown hair. Both came to a standstill when they saw him.

"Sorry, didn't know you had company. We'll head off."

"No. Come on in. Let me introduce you." Colton left the open door and strode over to Ioan, sliding his arm around Ioan's waist. "Jimmy, Dani, this is Ioan." Their eyes rounded as did their mouths, and Colton chuckled. "This is the first time I've ever seen them speechless."

"The English guy?" Jimmy finally said.

"Yes."

"Nice to meet you," Ioan said, holding out his shaky hand.

Jimmy took it in his and shook it before Dani took his place. "Nice to meet you, too. I've heard a lot about you." Dani cast a look at Colton, which Ioan couldn't decipher, but then turned her smile back to him. "Well, we'll be going as you've already got plans. We just came to see if you wanted to go out."

"Nah, I'm good. I'll catch up with you soon." Colton smiled at them as they left, closing the door behind them. "Now, where were we?"

His lips kissed a trail up Ioan's neck to just under his ear, where Colton had found an erogenous zone last time they were in this position. As he nibbled on the area, Ioan's knees trembled, and he clutched at the back of Colton's t-shirt as his eyes rolled back in his head. Colton pressed his hand against the front of Ioan's jeans, rubbing back and forth. Ioan pushed forward, moaning, craving more friction. Colton's mouth covered Ioan's, and he pulled them away from the wall, both stumbling towards the bedroom, not wanting to let go of each other.

Ioan's legs hit the bed, and he fell backwards with Colton on top, laughing when Colton impatiently yanked his jumper off. Ioan slid his hands under Colton's t-shirt, skimming his fingertips along his ribs to his nipples, then continuing until he could yank the material over Colton's head. His hands returned to Colton's body, and he hissed when Colton sucked a nipple into his mouth. Ioan's head dropped back, and Colton fumbled with Ioan's jeans before pulling them off completely.

Returning the favour, Ioan unfastened Colton's trousers and pushed them down, using his feet to lower them further. Colton slid them off and sank down over Ioan.

"God, Colton. Fuck me. Please!"

Their hips thrust against each other, their covered cocks rubbing together, heightening their pleasure. Colton kissed and licked his way down Ioan's stomach, sliding his fingers between the waistband of his boxers, then dragged them off. As soon as Ioan's cock was free, Colton swallowed him down.

"Fuck!" Ioan groaned as he tried to simultaneously pull Colton onto his cock and push him away. "Colton! Wait!"

Colton lifted off, leaning forward to kiss Ioan. "What's wrong?"

"I need you," Ioan panted. "Hard and fast."

Colton's gaze roamed Ioan's face. He dropped a kiss

onto Ioan's lips then sat up, shucking his boxers and grabbing the lube and a condom from the drawer. He kneeled between Ioan's spread thighs, smoothing his hands across Ioan's skin, leaving goosebumps in his wake. The lube bottle clicked open, and Ioan opened his eyes—he hadn't even realised he'd closed them.

Fingers rubbed against his hole, and Ioan watched Colton prepare him; the calloused fingers dragging against Ioan's entrance felt divine. Once he was taking three fingers, Colton rolled on a condom and slicked it before holding himself against Ioan's ass.

"You sure?"

Ioan nodded, biting his bottom lip. Colton lifted Ioan's legs over his shoulders, then Colton drove forward in a smooth yet sudden thrust. Ioan groaned and gripped Colton's forearms as Colton withdrew and slammed back in repeatedly. Getting what he asked for had never felt so good.

"Jesus, Ioan," Colton growled, jaw clenched.

Ioan lifted his head, wanting to kiss Colton. Almost bent in half, Ioan licked into Colton's mouth. Colton's hips were never still, thrusting and pounding Ioan into the mattress as their kiss continued. Pulling away, Colton held onto Ioan's legs and increased his speed. Ioan wrapped his hand around his cock and stroked in time with Colton's hips, his climax barrelling towards him.

"Oh, fuck, Colton! I'm nearly there!"

Colton changed his grip slightly and pegged Ioan's prostate, throwing Ioan over the edge. As he orgasmed, he saw, through narrowed eyes, Colton's face pinched in what could only be described as painful pleasure as he followed Ioan.

After Colton discarded the condom, Ioan wrapped himself around the naked man, pillowing his head on Colton's shoulder. Best decision ever.

Ioan stood in the airport, hating the thought of what was to come but knowing there was no other option. His anxiety was at an all-time high.

"I'll have to leave you here," Colton said quietly.

Ioan swallowed hard and turned to face Colton. "I'm gonna miss you."

Colton embraced Ioan, holding him tight against the body Ioan had gotten to know so well over the past few days. They had spent their days at the market with Ioan wandering around to see what knick-knacks he could buy for his friends and family, and their nights tangled up amongst the sheets. Everything had felt a little surreal.

It sure as heck didn't at that moment. It was all too real.

Two hands cupped his jaw as Ioan tried not to break down in tears. He'd been so sure it was the right decision to visit Colton, but this leaving him…was heart-breaking. How he was going to do this every year, he had no idea.

"I'll be with you in two weeks. That's all. I'll be there before you know it."

Colton kissed him, hard and deep, and Ioan clung to

him, not wanting to let go but needing to. Pulling away, he pressed their foreheads together. "Call and message me, okay. I'll let you know when I get back."

Colton nodded, dropping a kiss to his nose before stepping away and reaching for his coffee cup, which had been balanced precariously on Ioan's suitcase. "See you on the flipside." Colton's mouth quirked up, although Ioan could see the tension in the deepening lines on his face.

Ioan grasped his empty cup, lifting it in semblance of a toast, then turned and headed towards security. He couldn't bring himself to look back. He wasn't sure if he'd be able to leave again if he did. Two weeks. He could do that. It was only two weeks.

CHAPTER ELEVEN

COLTON

Two weeks was a fucking long time when you wanted to be with someone and couldn't. Every little thing felt like it took days instead of minutes, and Colton struggled to concentrate. He knew Ioan was upset about the distance between them, but Colton couldn't say anything to ease it.

When he finally got into the cab at the airport, he messaged Ioan straight away. Unfortunately, Ioan was working and hadn't been able to swap his shift, so Colton wouldn't see him until later that night. Ioan had invited Colton to stay with him for his trip, and Colton wasn't about to say no to an offer like that. Going to sleep and waking up next to Ioan for a week? Definite bonus.

At Ioan's house, he let himself in with the key Ioan had given him back in New York. Colton had been confused when Ioan had offered it, not understanding how Ioan would be able to get in his house until Ioan had confessed he'd brought the spare key with him just so he could give it to Colton. That had started a whole new round of lovemaking.

He left the suitcases at the bottom of the stairs and wandered around the house, grabbing a drink from the kitchen. The house was a lovely two-bedroom place in a seemingly nice neighbourhood.

Colton debated whether to go to Crush as he normally would or wait for Ioan to get home. Although he'd messaged Zak to let him know when he was arriving, they hadn't set a time or place to meet up. As it was so close to Christmas when he'd arrived—it would be Christmas Eve the following day—he was sure everyone would have plans already.

Checking his watch, he saw he still had just under three hours before Ioan would finish work. He decided to do his usual thing. Dragging his suitcases up the stairs, he went to the room they'd been in the previous year. Once he'd taken a shower and redressed, he called a cab and messaged Ioan while he was waiting for it to arrive.

I'm here, finally. I'm going to head to Crush for an hour, but I'll be back before you finish work. C x

He didn't expect a reply straight away and slipped his phone into his pocket. When the cab arrived, he wrapped himself up in his coat and headed out. The drive didn't take long, and before he knew it, he was entering his usual English haunt. Crush was the same as ever. Nothing had changed as far as he could see, apart from a couple of new faces behind the bar he hadn't seen last time. It was busier than he'd expected for a Monday, but it was Christmas, so that probably made a difference. The steady hum of loud conversation and background music was relaxing.

Taking a seat at the counter, he studied the room, trying to see if there was anyone he knew.

"What can I get you?"

Colton faced the young man and smiled. "I'll take a beer, thanks."

"Ooh, American. We don't see a lot of American people around here." The bartender looked young enough to still be at school, but he was obviously old enough to serve alcohol, which made him twenty-one… no, eighteen. UK laws were different.

"I come here every year. You're new, though." Colton was curious because he'd never seen a new face behind the bar in all the years he'd been coming. It was a bit of a shock.

"Not really new. I started July last year. You must've come in on my day's off last time." The guy placed the beer in front of Colton and held out his hand. "Charlie."

"Colton. Nice to meet you."

"Colton!"

He swung round on the stool when he heard a female voice he knew well enough now. When Analise threw her arms around him, he laughed and hugged her back.

"That's a nice greeting. How are you?"

"Oh, so much better now that I've seen you. I didn't think we were going to see you this year."

Colton grinned. "You can't escape me, sorry. Yeah, this year, I came a little later than usual."

"You'll have to come in tomorrow. We have a party planned. It will be great." Analise slid behind the bar.

"I'll see."

"You have better things to do than hang around with me?" Analise pouted, looking sad.

"Maybe." Colton grinned.

"Ooh. Who is he?"

"Is he that guy at the nursing home you mentioned last year?"

Colton turned at the second familiar voice. "Hey, Zak." He stood, gripping Zak's hand in his and leaning in for a hug.

"Nice to see you again. You've not changed."

Colton ran a hand over his head. "Why change perfection?"

Zak laughed, clapping him on the back. "So, is it the guy from the nursing home?"

Nodding slowly, Colton said, "Yeah. We're taking things slow, but I'm hoping to figure out where we're going. It's still in the early stages."

"Definitely come tomorrow, then. You can chill out with friends and have a drink," Analise said.

"Analise, give him a break." Charlie nudged her hip, and Analise swatted him away.

"What? I'm just being friendly. Anyway, he'd get to see a lot more people tomorrow. Josh will be here, and so will Kade and the usual crew." She turned to Colton. "Come on. Please?"

Colton shook his head. "Let me see. If I can be here, I'll be here."

"Yes!"

"She certainly knows how to twist people to her will," Zak remarked.

"Tell me about it." Colton drank some beer, pulling his phone out to check for any messages. He smiled when he saw Ioan had replied.

You can stay there if you like, and I'll meet you there? x

He chuckled as he sent one back.

Sure you want our reunion to be witnessed by the customers? x

He left his phone on the bar and turned to Zak. "Sorry."

Zak waved him away. "Don't worry. I can tell by the smile on your face who the message was from." He pointed over his shoulder. "Do you want to come and join us?"

"Yeah, sure. Depending on how Ioan replies, he might be coming here to meet me."

They headed over to the small cluster of tables where several guys sat laughing and talking. Colton grabbed a chair from a table next to them and sat beside Zak.

"Hey, guys. Remember this chap?" Zak squeezed his shoulder as Colton looked around at the faces.

"Hey, Colton. How're things?" Sean asked with a smile.

"Good, thanks. How are you?"

"Doing good."

"What're you talking about? You're doing better than

good, asshole." Max—having obviously not changed one bit in a year—pointed to the guy on the opposite side of Sean. "That there is Asher, and Sean's boyfriend. They're all sweet and lovey-dovey with each other."

Sean backhanded Max's chest. "Shut up. Just because you're jealous."

Colton chuckled but reached a hand forward to shake Asher's. "I see you've got your hands full."

"Yeah, they come as part of a package. Not much I can do about it," Asher deadpanned.

"Oi!"

Asher wrapped his arm around Sean's shoulders, grinning. "You know I don't mind."

"Well, while they're making up, let me do the introductions as Zak isn't." Max pursed his lips at Zak.

"I haven't had a chance." Zak snorted.

"So, this one of Asher's best friends, Trent," Max said. "His other best friend is at work."

"Nice to meet you," Colton said. He felt his phone buzz and slid it out of his pocket. "Sorry, excuse me a second."

Good point, but I don't mind. You're closer there than you are at home. And besides, I can give you a ride home on the bike. ;-) x

He had a very good point. Colton had never thought he would enjoy riding a motorbike as much as he found he did.

Deal. I'll see you here when you get here. I'm at the back of the bar with a group of friends. x

He pocketed his phone again and turned to Zak. "He's meeting me here."

"Great. Let's get you another drink, then."

Colton spent a very enjoyable couple of hours chatting with his friends and drinking beer. He had a nice buzz going by the time someone tapped him on the shoulder.

Lifting his face, he saw Ioan and scrambled from his chair. "Hey." He smiled.

"Hi." Ioan had a very adorable blush on his face as his gaze skipped to the occupants of the table before coming back to Colton.

Colton cupped Ioan's cheek, then slid his hand around the back of his head, dragging his mouth closer, taking his lips in a painfully sweet kiss. "I missed you," he whispered. Ioan wrapped his arms around Colton and nestled his face into Colton's neck as he held him tight. Ioan trembled in his arms, and Colton tightened his grip. "I'm here now."

Ioan squeezed him tighter for a moment, then pulled away. "I missed you, too."

Unable to help himself, Colton took Ioan's mouth with his own, sliding his tongue over Ioan's when he opened on a gasp. He grasped the back of Ioan's head, not wanting it to end, although something was telling him it needed to. He ignored it until a wolf-whistle split their bubble.

Colton pulled away, breathing erratically. He glanced

over his shoulder to see several grinning faces and shook his head. He pressed one more kiss to Ioan's mouth, then turned to the table. Clearing his throat, he addressed Ioan, "I don't know if you know anyone, but let me see if I get everyone's names right. Trent, Asher, Sean, Max, Zak." He pointed at each person as he spoke and pulled over a chair for Ioan to sit next to him.

"So, are you coming to the party tomorrow?" Max asked.

Colton glanced at Ioan. "Not sure," he said at the same time Ioan asked, "What party?"

"The Crush Christmas party, of course. Although we are also celebrating Tom and Ginny's baby," Max announced.

Colton raised his eyebrows. "Really? That's something I missed. Tom didn't even have a girlfriend when I last spoke to him."

"Yeah, they'd kept it quiet for a little while before going public with it. I think they were worried about the age gap." At Colton's questioning glance, he added, "There's nineteen years between them."

"It's doesn't matter the difference, so long as they're happy," Ioan commented.

"Exactly!" Max said.

Colton studied Ioan, seeing the black areas under his eyes. He squeezed his hands. "Hey, guys, we're going to head out."

They said their goodbyes and promised to let Zak know about the party, then exited into the fairly warm night. Ioan led the way to his bike, and they mounted, speeding off towards Colton's home for the next week.

He'd missed being on the bike, but he'd missed Ioan more.

Colton sat with his mother at his uncle's house, surrounded by family, wishing Ioan was with him. As much as he loved his family, he wanted to be able to share it with Ioan. They were nowhere close to meeting each other's family members, though. They hadn't even mentioned it to his mom.

The kids loved all the gifts that Colton had brought for them, a mixture of made gifts and bought this year. Thanks to Ioan letting him stay at his house, Colton had a little spare cash for extra special gifts. He'd bought his mother a glass dome with a rose in the middle, just like in the princess film, and she'd loved it.

Colton had given Ioan his gift that morning after waking him early with a Christmas present of Colton's mouth on his cock. Once Ioan was coherent again, Colton had held out the box, heart hammering. Ioan had smiled and ripped the paper off, revealing a wooden depiction of Ioan's bike. It had taken Colton weeks to get the intricate details done, but he'd managed it. He was really pleased with it, as was Ioan if the sex they'd had afterwards was any indication.

Diverting his mind to somewhere else to stop the rise of his cock in the middle of the family visit, Colton stood to get a drink. He thought back to the previous night when they'd gone to the Crush party. Ioan had been happy to go and visit; he'd had the day off work anyway, so they visited with everyone, saw Tom's new baby and met a host of other partners and friends along the way. Ioan had even invited Kyle and Nick, although only Kyle could make it. It was nice to have that sense of companionship in England, too.

"Why didn't you invite Ioan to come with us?"

His mother's voice had him coughing up the water he just tried to swallow, and he was glad he'd been near the sink. After he regained his breath, he stared at her. "What?"

"You should've invited Ioan. He is family now, after all."

Colton continued to gape at her.

She chuckled. "You're not a sneaky as you think. I have ears, you know."

Colton's eyes widened, and his cheeks flushed hot. "I…We…"

She waved her hand. "Let's head back to the nursing home. I want to see my potential son-in-law."

He stared after her, unable to say a word. Son-in-law. They hadn't been together that long. But as much as he denied her words, something took root inside him. A warm feeling that wouldn't abate.

When they arrived back, Colton saw Ioan hard at work, organising the dining room to get it ready for the Christmas meal.

His mother patted his hand. "Go and see him. I'm going back to my room to sit down."

"Let me take you…"

"No, I'll be fine. In fact, Laura can help me." She wandered over to Laura and disappeared around the corner with her.

Colton glanced back at Ioan, watching his sure, confident movements. He didn't want to startle him, so he made some noise as he headed towards him. Ioan lifted his gaze, his eyes brightening when he saw Colton. Colton felt lighter noticing Ioan was happy to see him.

"Is your mum okay?"

"Yeah. She's fine. She went back to her room to sit. Uncle Brian's family gets bigger each year, so it's a bit overwhelming."

Ioan continued to work as they spoke. "Sounds like fun, though."

"They're great, yes." Colton paused. "Can I help at all?"

Ioan hesitated, studying Colton's face. "Sure."

They worked alongside each other, getting the tables and cutlery ready for lunch. They didn't speak much, but it was a comfortable silence, not one that needed to be filled. Colton hadn't experienced that before.

"And we're finished," Ioan stated, standing with his hands on his hips.

Colton wanted nothing more than to stride over to him and kiss the air from his lungs, but he couldn't do that there. It was Ioan's place of work, and he refused to jeopardise his job. He could see it in Ioan's eyes, though. He wanted it, too.

CHAPTER TWELVE

IOAN

Christmas had been bittersweet. Ioan managed to get some time off work while Colton was there, so they spent a couple of days visiting the sights around Cambridge and going on a longer journey on the bike, allowing Colton to really feel the power. They'd hired some bicycles and travelled around the tourist spots, like the churches and colleges, and along the River Cam. This was in between the visits to see Rose.

Colton had spent the whole of Boxing Day with Rose, showering her with attention and spoiling her rotten for her birthday while Ioan worked his shift. She'd been in good spirits the whole time Colton had been there, which was fantastic.

All in all, their time had been wonderful.

Ioan tried to ignore the looming darkness over their week. He disregarded the way his stomach rolled, the way he felt on edge, the way his tears felt constantly close to overflowing. He refused to think about what would happen when Colton left. Burying his head in the sand was not the best way to do things, but it was the only way Ioan could give Colton a good time.

In the middle of the night, when he was wide awake, Ioan let his thoughts run free but kept a tight lid on his emotions. He thought of all the things that went wrong with Axel and how he had no idea anything was amiss. He thought about how he and Colton would work with so much distance between them. Every time, he was unable to see their future.

As the day of Colton's departure drew nearer, Ioan could feel the tension building between them. Their love-making was more intense, more frantic. Their kisses harder and deeper. But nothing as desperate as the morning of his departure.

Ioan woke when Colton wrapped his mouth around his dick. His morning wood appreciated the attention, and Ioan groaned in anticipation. Despite being sore from the previous days' activities—both sexual and non-sexual—he was eager for more. The sensation of Colton's mouth alternately sucking and licking along his length had him closer than he wanted to be so soon.

Ioan reached a hand down to cup Colton's head, fingertips dragging across the short strands as he slid the sheet off them to reveal Colton's flushed face and glassy eyes. The sight was so hot, Ioan choked out an order to stop. Colton paused but didn't pull off.

"Fuck! I'm going to come if you keep doing that. Not yet," he croaked.

Colton slid him out of his mouth but gripped the back of Ioan's thighs and lifted them, baring Ioan's hole.

Ioan groaned as Colton's tongue licked from his ass to his balls. Colton bit at the globes of Ioan's cheeks, then pressed his tongue against his hole, licking and teasing it until Ioan's movements were uncontrollable. When Colton's tongue entered the ring, Ioan moaned, curling himself forward for more, but Colton retreated.

"I need more!"

Colton crawled over the bed to the table, reaching in the drawer for a condom and lube, but Ioan couldn't resist the sight of Colton kneeling with his cock so close and swallowed him down. Grunting, Colton straightened as Ioan's mouth laved the swollen head before sinking his mouth. Colton's hands rested on the back of Ioan's head, and his hips began to pump. Ioan kept his head still, allowing Colton to fuck his mouth.

"Ah! Fuck!"

With his hands on Colton's hips, Ioan could feel Colton trembling, trying to hold back. The wet sounds of Colton taking what he needed was an aphrodisiac and made Ioan's dick leak more precome.

"Ah!" Colton pulled away, breathing hard. He kissed Ioan, hard and deep as he moved between Ioan's legs. Kneeling back up, Colton's attention was on his hands as he lubed his fingers. Ioan didn't think he'd need much prep since they'd been extremely active in the past few days.

Sinking one finger inside Ioan, Colton thrust, carefully but quickly preparing him. Ioan watched through narrowed eyes as Colton rolled on the condom and slicked it up before resting it against Ioan's entrance. Colton lifted Ioan's legs to his shoulders and pushed in firmly, bottoming out within seconds. This was Colton's favourite position.

"Jesus! Fuck!" Ioan gripped the sheets below him, his mouth wide open as Colton settled into place. Ioan panted, adjusting to Colton's size. Their gazes met, and they stilled. Colton leaned down, bending Ioan in half as he reached for a kiss. Their tongues met lazily, and Colton thrust his hips minutely. Not nearly enough for Ioan.

His legs started to ache, so he moved them, crossing his ankles around Colton's back once Colton had repositioned his arms. Much better. Still seated inside Ioan, Colton slid his hands and forearms under Ioan's back, holding him close. Ioan wrapped his arms around Colton's neck and pulled him in for a kiss.

The kiss was lazy to begin with, tongues sliding against each other until Colton bit Ioan's lip. When he soothed it with his tongue, his hips withdrew a little and drove back in.

Wrapped as tight as he was around Colton, Ioan's cock didn't need any added stimulation to the friction it was receiving between their bodies. Colton pulled back, but Ioan didn't want him to leave. Colton leaned down and bit Ioan's lip again before breaking Ioan's hold and sliding his hands across Ioan's ribs. The change of position was delicious especially since Colton drove harder into him. Ioan reached one hand above him, resting his palm against the headboard, adding some resistance to Colton's movements, while his other hand stroked his cock.

"Oh, god!" Ioan's eyes rolled back in his head when Colton lifted Ioan's ass off the bed.

Gripping Ioan's hips, Colton slammed into him, hitting his prostate with every plunge.

"Fucking hell!" Colton let go and braced a hand beside Ioan's chest, cupping the back of Ioan's neck with the other. "I'm gonna come."

Ioan's hand stroked faster. "Come for me, Colton," he growled as thick ropes of come decorated his chest.

Colton groaned and dropped onto Ioan's chest, his face burrowing into Ioan's neck even as his hips continued to snap forward as he orgasmed. Ioan felt Colton's teeth in his neck, not hard but unrelenting, as Colton's hips slowed their rhythm.

Ioan enfolded Colton in his arms and legs, not wanting them to move ever again. He had no idea how long they lay together, but Colton lifted off with a grimace. The stickiness of Ioan's come had solidified slightly, making his chest feel tacky and disgusting.

"I have to go if I want to see Mom before I leave." Colton pressed a kiss to Ioan's lips and slid off the bed. "I'm just going to have a quick shower."

Ioan watched as Colton left the room. He rubbed his hands over his face and rolled onto his stomach, hiding his face in the pillows. The pillows that smelled of Colton and him. Inhaling deeply, he climbed off the bed, not bothering to join Colton in the shower. He'd grab one after Colton's flight had left. Using wipes he had in the room, he cleaned his chest and cock as best he could.

As he slid on his jeans, Colton entered with a towel

wrapped around his waist, drying his hair with another. Ioan glanced over, and Colton paused. "Are you okay?"

Ioan swallowed against the lump in his throat. He shook his head, then pulled a t-shirt over his head. "No, I'm not."

"I know this won't be easy, but I believe we can make it work."

"How?" Ioan turned to face him, resting back against the drawers with his arms crossed over his chest. He couldn't help the irritation that bled into his tone.

"We'll message and call, use video chat where we can. We'll fly across the ocean when we're able to. If not, I'll see you when I come for Christmas."

Ioan huffed and averted his gaze to the window. "I barely managed two weeks, Colton. How the hell can I manage a year?"

Colton stepped close and cupped Ioan's jaw. "Hey, both of us are in the same position. We will manage; we just need to communicate with each other."

"Communicate? That's all we'll have, Colton. Words. What about when you need comforting or when I need you to hold me? How's that going to work?"

Colton sighed. "I don't know, Ioan. We'll work it out as we go."

Ioan pulled away and stalked to the window, staring at nothing. "It killed me thinking about you so far away. I had no idea what you were doing."

There was silence, then Colton retorted, "*What* I was doing? Or *who* I was doing?"

Ioan heard rustling and peered over his shoulder, seeing Colton pulling on his clothes, his movements sharp and fast. Neither said anything. Colton finished dressing and packed the final few things in his suitcases. After pocketing his phone and wallet, he paused before exiting the bedroom.

"It's called trust, Ioan. You should try it." With those words, he left. Ioan followed Colton's footsteps in his mind until the front door closed quietly.

Ioan sat on the bed, dropping his head into his shaking hands. He couldn't see any way they could last. He'd been through every scenario he could think of and nothing worked. The stress of it all would be too much for Ioan; he knew that because Axel had made sure Ioan would never trust anyone like that again. He couldn't see a future for him and Colton when they were so far apart, and neither wanted to leave their respective country.

Despite the reasonable chance that Colton didn't want to see him again, Ioan couldn't let him leave without saying goodbye properly. Even if they never spoke after this, Ioan didn't want Colton to be by himself when he left. He finished getting ready, grabbed his things and headed to his bike.

The ride to the airport went by quickly. After checking his watch to see he was early, Ioan grabbed a drink from the small coffee shop, then trudged towards the security gates to wait.

He had no idea how long he'd been standing there when he saw Colton heading through the crowd. Ioan hustled forward to intercept him before he could reach the place where Ioan couldn't follow. Colton's expression was drawn, making him look several years older, and when he noticed Ioan, his face tightened, and his jaw clenched.

"What?" Colton bit out.

"I didn't want you to leave without saying goodbye."

Colton snorted without humour. "I thought we'd said enough."

Ioan swallowed. "I'm sorry. I know I—"

"Do you know what, Ioan? Save it. I don't want to hear anymore. I can't keep doing this back and forth with you. You need to make up your mind once and for all, but you're a coward."

Tears threatened to overflow, but Ioan refused to let them. Through blurring eyes, he whispered, "Maybe," then turned and walked away, throwing the drink in a bin as he passed. It was only as he fired up his bike, he realised he still hadn't said goodbye.

On the journey home, Ioan could barely hold back his emotions. He knew he'd done the right thing. Breaking it off with Colton was the best choice for them both. Colton could get on with his life in New York, and Ioan could carry on with his as he had before. Three years of Christmas celebrations ran through his head, the back and forth they had done, the good times, then the two weeks Ioan had been without him despite talking to him daily. Ioan couldn't spend a year doing that. He couldn't go all that time without touching him, holding him, wanting him close. It was better to forget and move on.

He stumbled into the house, limbs heavy and tiredness dragging his movements, and he decided to go back to bed. He didn't have to go to work. He put his keys on the table by the door and saw a single key sitting there. The reality of his decision crashed into him. Throwing the key he'd given Colton across the room, he sank to the floor, gripping his hair, and cried.

He woke, curled up on the floor by his front door, and it took a moment for him to figure out why. Emotions threatened to overwhelm him again, but he pushed them down. Gritty eyes made him head for the bathroom, and as he waited for the water to warm up, he studied his reflection. Apart from being puffy and red from crying, he looked the same except for his eyes. His eyes showed his devastation. His eyes advertised his grief. His eyes promoted his despair.

Didn't everyone say the eyes were the windows to the soul?

If it were true, Ioan was in trouble.

CHAPTER THIRTEEN

COLTON

2020

Colton had spent the first half of the year in a downward spiral. It had taken an intervention from Dani and Jimmy to show him what he was doing to himself: fucking and drinking his way through New York was not the best medicine. He'd finally come back to himself and felt much better for it. At least he could look at himself in the mirror now.

As he set up for the Union Square Holiday Market, he couldn't help the wave of anticipation of potentially seeing Ioan even as he brushed it aside as soon as he acknowledged it.

They hadn't spoken at all in the last year, except for one message from Ioan on Colton's birthday. Colton had sent back his thanks, but that was it. He still felt guilty for calling Ioan a coward. He shouldn't have said it, but he'd been angry. Having had the chance to calm down since his spiral had upturned, he no longer held Ioan to blame for their breakup. Colton should have seen the signs, especially with how much he knew Ioan had been hurt by his ex-boyfriend. That didn't excuse him completely because Ioan should've said something sooner than he did, but Colton could understand it.

"Colton!" He lifted his gaze to Jazz, his market stall neighbour. "Are you going out with us tonight?"

"Where are you going?"

"We're grabbing something to eat. You in?"

Colton couldn't think of a reason to decline; he wasn't sure he wanted to. "Yeah. Let me know where and when, and I'll be there."

His stall had been doing as well as it had the previous year despite his issues at the beginning of the year, and he'd decided not to expand any further for the moment. He had plenty of stock to last him through the season, meaning he had a bit of a break from working hard every evening. He had a few custom orders for small wooden toys, which needed to be ready for Christmas, but they wouldn't take him too long to make.

By the time he entered the restaurant Jazz had told him they were meeting at, Colton had decided he was going to let everything go and just have fun. He knew a fair few of the other stallholders now that he'd had a place on the market for several years. Some of them were like him, following the different markets around New York throughout the year, and some did only the Union Square one.

He greeted everyone and ordered himself a drink before sitting and joining in the conversation. The food was amazing, and the company could only have been better if Dani and Jimmy had been with him. They had plans the following night, just a movie night with a take-out, but he was looking forward to it.

The later the hour became, the louder the music was. According to Jazz, this place was mellow while it was still in restaurant mode, but when it closed its kitchen, it turned into more of a club. If Colton had known that, he would've left earlier.

One of his colleagues stepped closer, leaning in to be heard over the music. "Would you like to dance?"

Colton studied the man. He was shorter than Colton by a good few inches; he barely reached Colton's chin, but he was cute. He had a little button nose that turned up at the end slightly, pale skin and a wide smile with dark red lips. If Colton remembered correctly, his name was Travis. Colton planned to leave, but with Travis's question, he decided to throw caution to the wind. He wasn't reverting back to his early months of the year; he was just going to have a dance with someone he liked the appearance of. Nothing else would happen.

"Sure." Colton placed his beer on the bar and his hand on Travis's lower back, allowing Travis to lead the way.

Once they were swallowed up by the crowd, bodies pressing in from all sides, Travis slid his hands up Colton's arms and around his shoulders as their bodies fell into the beat. Colton's hands rested on Travis's hips, the sway of the man's hips hypnotising. Several songs passed before Colton pulled back.

"I need a drink," he said into Travis's ear.

They headed back to the bar, giving Colton some distance to breathe without inhaling the sweat-soaked air. He plucked his shirt from his chest a few times to cool him down, though it didn't make much of a difference because he was covered in sweat himself.

Leaning one elbow against the bar and facing Travis, Colton said, "You're a good dancer."

"Thanks. I did dance at college for no other reason than I love to dance." Travis smiled. "It didn't exactly fit in with my business degree, but I didn't care."

"What made you decide to do a market stall if you have a business degree?" Colton ordered them two beers while he waited for Travis's answer.

"I wanted to see a business grow from the ground up, see how much effort someone needed to put into it to make a decent income. I also wanted to see the different variables that cropped up, such as weather, state issues, things like that. I could've started a business in a nice cushy office, but I love the outdoors. It seemed a good fit."

Colton was impressed. "If you don't mind me asking, how old are you?"

Travis grinned. "I'm twenty-six."

Older than he'd thought. "And have you figured out all your calculations yet?"

Travis shook his head. "No, there are plenty more things that need to be figured out before I decide whether to carry on with what I'm doing or do something else.

I'm making enough money to live on while I make my discoveries, so I'm happy to continue as I am for now." Travis sipped his beer. "What about you?"

Colton thought about his answer. "In the beginning, and we're talking around twelve years now, it was a reminder of what my dad and I enjoyed doing before he died. Making wooden items, that is. It was a way of still being close to him, I suppose." Colton swallowed some beer. "I guess I fell in love with the community, the workload, the environment. It filled something I needed filling at the time."

"And now?" Travis asked.

"What do you mean?" Colton frowned.

"Well, you said it filled something *at the time*. That means it either doesn't need filling now, or it is full enough. Are you going to continue with the market?" Travis leaned against the bar, resting his head on his fist as he looked at Colton as if he had not pulled the rug from under Colton's feet.

Colton stared to the side, unable to answer the not-so-innocent question.

"Sorry. I didn't mean to put a downer on the night."

"No! It's okay. I just hadn't realised…" *that I was done*, he finished silently.

Colton thought about all the things he'd been doing since he'd gotten his act together again. He'd made enough stock for the season and then stopped, whereas every other year, he had continued so he had more stock for the following year. He'd thought about the custom orders he had and the fact he had declined any more. For all intents and purposes, it appeared Colton was shutting up shop.

A hand on his forearm brought his attention back to Travis. "Are you okay?"

Colton smiled and nodded. "Yeah, I'm good."

And he was. The idea of not doing another stall after his season finished was…soothing. He had no idea what he would do if he was definitely going to go down that road, but maybe he could bring it up with Dani and Jimmy and see what they had to say about it.

"Thank you, Travis. I had a great night."

Travis bit his lip. "Would you like to continue it?" he asked hesitantly.

Colton gave him a small smile. "At any other time, I would've said yes, but I'm on the wrong side of a relationship and need to get my head together. You're a great guy, Travis." He leaned forward and kissed Travis's cheek.

"Thanks, Colton. I'll see you around."

"Definitely." Colton winked and weaved through the hordes of people, shivering as he exited into the freezing night air. He quickly donned his coat and zipped it up, yanking his hat onto his head. The restaurant was not far from his apartment, so he decided to walk the distance. It gave him a chance to think more about Travis's observations.

"I'm thinking of packing it in," Colton said into the silence.

The three of them were sitting in front of his TV, watching a movie marathon and eating pizza. He hadn't planned on blurting it out, but it had been on his mind since Travis had made his innocent comment, and he needed to talk it through.

"Packing what in?" Jimmy asked, a pizza slice halfway to his mouth.

"The market."

Dani twisted in her seat to face him fully. "What's made you decide this?"

Colton inhaled. "I don't think it was a conscious decision." He explained his thoughts about how he'd been slowly dwindling what he was making without realising it. "What are your thoughts?"

"Why now?" Dani asked. She was sat cross-legged on the sofa next to him, her face a mixture of confusion and…something else Colton couldn't identify.

"Why not now?" Colton couldn't answer that question either. He had no idea what made this year the year he was making significant changes, which could be problematic to his earnings in a short while.

Colton watched as Dani fidgeted and bit her lip. He raised his eyebrows at her uncharacteristic show of uneasiness. "What are you thinking, Dani?" he asked.

"Okay, don't be…" she waved her hand over him, "*you* for a moment and hear me out." Colton nodded despite finding her words amusing. "Do you think you are considering a change of address?" she said slowly.

Colton stared at her in confusion. "What do you mean?"

Dani glanced at Jimmy, though Colton couldn't see what passed between them.

"What she's trying to say is, are you planning on moving to England?" Jimmy inquired.

Colton stared at him, mind whirling. Was he? Why now? His brain raced, searching for answers. "Not consciously," he replied.

"And now?" Dani's question echoed that of Travis's the previous night.

"I have no idea."

"Okay, you're probably going to hate me for this, but I think you should go. I think it's something you actually want to do, and not just because your mom is there. This past year has been hell for you. You will never know if it was a good idea or not unless you try." Dani smiled at him.

"And if it doesn't work out?"

"Come back."

She said it as if it was something so simple. As if he could just up and leave his whole life. He couldn't reconcile the idea that he'd been subconsciously planning to move to England. Other than his mother and his dad's family, there was nothing there for him.

Ioan.

Colton shook his head. Ioan would be with someone else by now. He was too much of a nice guy to be single for long.

"What's the worst that could happen?" Jimmy asked.

"I could waste all my money moving my whole life

across the Atlantic and be dirt poor," Colton deadpanned.

"Well, you're already dirt poor, so it wouldn't be much of a change." Jimmy laughed when Dani threw a cushion at him.

"Actually, I'm not," Colton admitted.

"Not what?"

"Poor." They both gaped at him as if he had two heads. He chuckled. "Business has been booming. Apart from paying for bills and for the flights to see Mom, I hardly spend anything. I'd say I have enough for me to live without working for around six months or so."

"Why are you still living in this shit hole, then?" Jimmy asked.

"Why change when this serves me fine."

Dani laughed. "You're unbelievable."

After they'd left, Colton cleaned up and headed to bed. As he lay there in the dark, staring at the ceiling, he thought about what his life could be like in England. He'd have to get a regular job, find somewhere to live, have all of his things shipped over. It was too much hassle. Packing up and leaving the place he called home and inserting himself in a country he hardly knew anything about was not his idea of fun. He'd figure out his way here, in New York. Something was sure to grab his attention soon.

One thing he had decided, though. His market stall was closing. Whether he closed his woodwork business completely was another thing.

When he finished his final market, he had several colleagues circling his stall. They cheered for him as he closed the final box with the remainder of his stock. He went around, chatting with the men and women who had become like family to him. The lady who owned the hot drink stall had made them all some hot chocolate to keep them warm while they said goodbye.

When Colton saw Travis, he pulled him in for a hug. "Thank you."

Travis pulled back with a quizzical expression on his face. "For what?"

"For making me realise what was right in front of me."

"And what was right in front of you?"

"The rest of my life."

Colton went home content, although a little sad that it was the end of an era. When he turned up at home, Dani and Jimmy were there to assist him in dragging the boxes up the stairs. He ordered takeaway as a thank you to them for helping him. He had nothing planned that evening except relaxing with his two best friends. They ended up having a *Die Hard* marathon since none of them had to be up early the following morning, and Dani and Jimmy ended up staying over. Colton offered Jimmy his bed—there was no way he'd fit on Colton's sofa— Dani took the sofa, and Colton used his sleeping bag.

He couldn't sleep, though. He stared into the darkness as he tried to figure out all the different emotions trickling through him: excitement, anxiety, and determination, to name a few, but mostly, peace with his decision. It wasn't the easiest decision he had ever made but he was sure it would turn out to be the best.

Flipping onto his side, he smiled. When one door closes, another one opens. He hoped.

CHAPTER FOURTEEN

IOAN

Thanksgiving had become synonymous with Colton, Ioan realised. Even though it wasn't celebrated in England, Ioan was aware of when it was; after all, he'd spent the last two years in New York around the holiday.

Ioan's mood was unpredictable. He was never horrible to the residents or staff at work, but he also wasn't his usual bubbly self. He couldn't help it. As much as he'd tried to get over Colton, and even though he'd been the one to break things off, he couldn't help except want him, need him.

He'd been on a number of dates during the past year, but each one had been terrifyingly boring. Ioan felt a deep ache inside every time one of the guys tried to kiss him goodnight. It was as if he was cheating when, in fact, he wasn't. His heart wasn't listening. After months of dissecting every possible scenario in which he and Colton could be together, he had been unable to find a way to work through his issues with the long-distance, so Ioan ended up doing nothing.

The message he'd sent on Colton's birthday had been replied to with a thank you, but nothing more. If that didn't give Ioan an idea of where Colton's feelings were, nothing would. How could Ioan blame him? He was the one to push Colton away time after time. Colton's arrival date loomed closer, and Ioan had no idea how to act around him. Did they ignore their past relationship and try to make things bearable, or did they talk about it and clear the air?

"Are you listening, Ioan?"

Ioan returned his attention to Laura, who raised her eyebrows at him. "Sorry, Laura."

Her forehead creased as she leaned forward. "Are you okay?"

Staring at a point in front of him, he wasn't sure what to say. "Could I take some time off over Christmas this year?" He had no idea where the words had come from, but he refused to take them back. Maybe this was what he needed—a break from his usual routine.

"Are you sure?" Laura looked at him, concern easily showing on her face.

He nodded. "Yeah. I need a break."

Laura sighed and turned to her computer. "You could have any time between the twenty-second of December until the third of January if that's any good?"

"Can I take all of it?"

Laura stared at him, her face expressionless. Ioan grew uncomfortable under her gaze but refused to fidget. She nodded slowly. "Sure."

"Thanks."

"I would need you to be on call, though. But only if someone goes down ill."

"No problem."

"Are you certain you want to do this? You usually enjoy working Christmas." Laura leaned back and crossed her arms over her chest.

"I'm sure."

As Ioan left her office, he headed back to work. Having almost two weeks off would give him a chance to figure out a lot of stuff and hopefully start the new year in a better frame of mind.

Having finally finished his last shift of the year, Ioan said goodbye to everyone and headed towards his bike. As soon as the engine rumbled beneath his thighs, he relaxed, closing his eyes and taking a deep breath. It was three days before Christmas, so he'd be able to decorate his house for a change. He hadn't decorated much in previous years because he had hardly ever been at home for it, but this year, he would be. He needed to visit the supermarket to get more things, but first, he would check what he already had and make a list.

Plan made, he roared out of the car park.

Even with the time he'd booked off, he had no plans to visit his dad because his dad had already arranged his usual trip with his friends and wouldn't be around. He was not a person for celebrating, not since Ioan had been a kid, anyway.

Kyle and Nick, though. He'd had no choice with what they had planned for him. As soon as he told them he wasn't working, they'd arranged for them to go out for nights out. Both were busy tonight and tomorrow, thankfully, so Ioan would be able to get things done around the house first. After that, though, he was in their hands.

Locking his front door behind him, he stood in the hallway, staring at the bare canvas that was his home. Bare of Christmas decorations that was. Jogging up the stairs, Ioan took a quick shower to clean off his work mode, then climbed into the attic where he stored the things he didn't use very often. He found two boxes labelled Christmas and lugged them down into the living room. Sitting on the sofa, he opened each of the boxes to see what he had.

Not much was the answer.

Checking his watch, he decided to do the supermarket run in the morning, and instead, went to make dinner.

As the scent of frying bacon filled the kitchen, Ioan realised how strange it was to not have anything that needed to be done. His routine had always been set by what his shifts were in the coming days. With a wide-open calendar, he felt a little adrift. Glancing around the kitchen, he decided some home improvements would help to pass the time. He'd always wanted to paint the kitchen, having never really been fond of the blue. Despite the cold weather, he should be able to do it, and it should dry fairly quickly.

Putting it on his to-do list, he settled down in front of the TV with his food and switched on the series he had been wanting to watch for a while. When he finally switched it off after five episodes, he was exhausted. He hadn't planned on watching so many, but it pulled him in.

Two days later, he finished the first season and was eager to start the second, but he needed to get ready for his night out. If he didn't turn up, one of them would come and drag him out, kicking and screaming.

Dressed in dark blue jeans, a black shirt and black boots, he entered a bar he'd not been in before. Kyle knew he was on his way, so hopefully, he'd be watching out for Ioan to arrive. Being the day before Christmas Eve, it was busy, and Ioan had to elbow his way through the crowds as he searched the tables—that was one thing Kyle had told him, that they'd managed to get a table. Kyle had neglected to say where the table was.

"Ioan! Over here!"

Ioan glanced to his right and saw Nick standing, waving at him.

"Whose idea was it to come out on a night like this," Ioan chuckled as he sat, grabbing the beer Nick pushed towards him. "Thanks." He took a swig, wiping his forehead. The heat from the sheer number of people certainly kept the chill away.

"His," Nick answered, pointing at Kyle.

Ioan grinned. "So, what's been going on with you two since I saw you last?"

Due to their jobs, none of them had been able to sync their calendars well enough to meet up before tonight; therefore, it had been several weeks since they'd seen each other.

"Working," they both said in unison.

"Well, alright, then." He'd always thought that if Kyle and Nick had been into other guys, they would've made the perfect couple. They were always in sync with each other. Knowing they wouldn't take too kindly to where his thoughts had gone, he schooled his expression and quirked a brow. "When are you guys back at work?"

Nick pursed his lips. "I'm back tomorrow, but only for half a day, then I'm off until Tuesday."

"I'm not back until the fourth of January." Kyle knocked his bottle against Ioan's in celebration before nudging Nick's shoulder, a smile on his face. "Chin up. We'll party enough for you, too."

Nick pressed his palm against Kyle's face and pushed him away. "Shut up, asshole. Maybe I'll call in sick."

"Don't be stupid. You'd never get away with that," Kyle countered.

"Why not?"

"Because you're never sick," Ioan interrupted. "You have the best immune system I've ever known."

Nick groaned.

"Never mind." Kyle patted him on the shoulder. "Let's have fun tonight. It can keep you going through the pain of tomorrow."

"You mean him still being drunk tomorrow will help him get through the day, don't you?" Ioan chuckled.

"Depends how drunk we can get him." Kyle winked.

All were sufficiently inebriated to need a taxi home, although Ioan was more sober than the other two. Once the taxi stopped at Kyle's house, Ioan decided to crash there instead of carrying on. Nick might need help getting up the following morning.

"I'm so sorry, Ioan. I know you wanted time away, but it will just be for the remainder of Susie's shift," Laura said.

"It's fine, don't worry. You'll have to give me an hour or so because I'm only just heading home."

"Sure. I'll cover her until you can get here. Thanks, Ioan. And I'm sorry again."

When they hung up, Ioan sighed. So much for time off. He couldn't begrudge her asking. Susie had been taken to hospital with suspected appendicitis; therefore, it was no one's fault. He'd just finished putting Nick in a taxi to work, and he hadn't even been home yet.

"Kyle? I have to go. I've been called into work."

"Please don't shout," Kyle whispered, holding his head.

Ioan laughed and placed two bottles of water and paracetamol in front of him. "Drink and sleep it off. I'll check on your later."

Grabbing his coat, he stepped out of the door and headed towards the taxi that was waiting for him. He'd been surprisingly pain-free since he woke, but he wasn't going to tempt fate by saying it aloud. When he finally walked back into his house, he didn't relax, though he wanted to. He climbed the stairs and jumped into the shower before drying off and dressing in his work clothes.

Ioan swallowed hard at the knowledge he might bump into Colton. He knew he'd arrived a couple of days before, but hopefully, Ioan would be too busy to worry about it. By the time he got to the nursing home, he only had five hours to work before Susie's shift ended. He'd be able to stay out of Colton's way for that amount of time, surely.

Going about his work, he kept an eye on his surroundings at all times. He wanted to be able to go in a different direction if he saw Colton coming. Alright, he wanted to hide. No amount of preparation would be enough to stop any reaction if Ioan did see him.

"Ioan, could you take this paperwork to Marie, please?" Laura handed him several files. "I need to go and see John."

"Sure thing."

Ioan pivoted and headed back towards reception, passing the files to Marie with a smile before someone spun him around and pressed him against the reception desk. He didn't have a chance to see who it was before the person's—man's—mouth was on his. Ioan inhaled through his nose as he became lightheaded. As soon as the scent hit him, he relaxed, sliding his hands up the man's arms to his shoulders. Then, he realised what he was doing and pushed against the man's chest.

Staring into the dove-grey eyes he knew so well, Ioan tried to gather his thoughts. "What...?" He licked his lips. "What are you doing?" he whispered.

"I can't live without you, Ioan," Colton decreed, hands cupping Ioan's face tenderly. "I'm here to stay."

"What?" Ioan felt shock course through him.

"I'm moving…I've moved to Cambridge. All my belongings are either here or on their way."

"But why?" Ioan didn't understand what Colton was doing. Colton hadn't wanted to leave New York.

"There's nothing holding me in New York, only what I thought I wanted." Colton brushed his thumb across Ioan's bottom lip. "But I want you more."

Ioan stared at Colton, trying to understand what the hell was happening. "But your market?"

"I closed it down."

"What about all your orders and stock?"

"The orders I had were done and delivered. The stock is being sent here, but there wasn't much left."

"What about Dani and Jimmy?"

Colton chuckled. "They'll survive without me. It gives them an excuse to visit the UK, anyway."

Ioan's heart started racing. He didn't want to believe it. "You're here to stay? In Cambridge?"

Colton smiled and nodded.

"Promise?"

"Promise."

Ioan flung his arms around Colton's neck and kissed him. He opened his mouth for Colton's questing tongue, sinking into him, and only pulled away when he heard people clapping around them. Then, he remembered where he was. He glanced around, seeing residents and staff alike surrounding them, smiling and cheering. Ioan was mortified and buried his head in Colton's neck while Colton's chuckle reverberated through his chest.

"It took you two long enough," Rose said from beside them. Ioan glanced at her, biting his lip. "I didn't think either of you would get your heads out of your asses to figure it out." She rolled her eyes, the juvenile response seeming strange on her smiling face.

"We got there in the end, Mom." Colton grinned.

"That you did." She looked at them fondly.

"Right. Now that's sorted…Ioan, you can go home," Laura said.

"But what about Susie's shift?"

"I can cover Susie's shift, Ioan. I'm surprised you fell for that." Laura smiled.

"You set me up!" Ioan narrowed his gaze at her.

"It was all for the good of your health." She smirked.

Colton slid his arm around Ioan's waist, pulling him close. "I put her up to it, sorry."

Ioan gazed at him. "Payback's a bitch."

Colton grinned. "I wouldn't expect anything less."

Ioan cupped Colton's jaw and kissed him chastely. "Glad you're here."

"There's nowhere else I'd rather be."

CHAPTER FIFTEEN

COLTON

When he had decided to up and leave New York, Colton was nervous as hell. He didn't tell anyone in England except Laura because he didn't want people getting their hopes up and then have something stop him from leaving when he said he would. After Laura had told him Ioan had taken the whole of Christmas off, Colton had been sad it had come down to Ioan avoiding him. It had made Colton second guess his plans.

His belongings would take a little while to come since his decision had been a last-minute thing. He'd only decided two weeks prior to flying in for Christmas, so packing up his apartment had been a rush job. Luckily, Dani and Jimmy had been a huge help, and they were back home—no, back in New York, helping with the finishing touches of his move.

When Colton had approached Laura about moving to England, she had been a little uneasy until he'd explained he wouldn't be forcing Ioan into anything Ioan didn't want to be part of. She'd been on board since then and had helped him concoct the plan to get Ioan to at least see him so Colton could apologise.

Colton hadn't expected to kiss Ioan before even saying hello, but he hadn't been able to resist, and Ioan had melted into him—at least, at first. It was only as Ioan pushed him away that he wondered if he would receive a slap for it.

Wrapping his arms tighter around Ioan's waist as they swerved through the traffic towards Ioan's house, Colton felt content. There was still a lot to discuss, but for now, things were going well.

As they climbed off, Colton saw Ioan sneaking glances at him as if checking he really was there. They walked into the house in silence, removing their coats and shoes before Colton faced Ioan.

"Are you okay?"

"I don't know." Ioan's response was quiet, unsure. "This year has been the worst year of my life. I won't survive going through it again. I know it was my decision to end things between us, but it…hurt. A lot." Ioan cleared his throat and drifted over to the sofa to sit. "If you have any reservations about this…about us, you need to tell me now. I can't go through it again and come out the other side unscathed."

Colton's heart broke. He knew exactly how Ioan felt because he had been going through the same things. He stepped forward, kneeling at Ioan's feet as he laid his heart on the line. "I'm all in. Everything. I want it all. My year has been shit, too, and I never want to go through that again if I can help it. You knew last year what I wanted, but I understand why you couldn't commit then." He exhaled roughly, shaking his head. "I hadn't even realised I was going to be moving here until two weeks ago."

Ioan gasped, "What?"

Colton chuckled. "Yeah, although I had decided to shut down my market, I had no idea what I planned to do afterwards. Even the shutting of the stall was an unconscious decision at first. Dani was the one who made me face myself."

Hands cupped his face. "I can't believe you're here," Ioan whispered.

"I'm here as long as you'll have me."

"Where are you living now?" Ioan asked, letting go of Colton's face, much to his disappointment.

"I'm at the hotel for a few weeks until I find a place. I wondered if you could help me?" Colton quirked his mouth. "I have no idea about houses around here."

"Of course, I can." Ioan hesitated. "If you want… you could stay here instead of the hotel until you find somewhere?"

As much as Colton wanted that, he didn't want to push Ioan too fast. "I would love that, but how about we give it a couple of days and see where we are? I refuse to crowd you when you definitely have things to think about."

Ioan stared at him, gaze roaming around his face. "I don't need to think about anything. I trust you." He licked his lips. "You might not trust me, though." His face fell as he looked away, sitting back in the seat.

"Why?" Colton rose and sat next to him, grabbing his hand.

"I'm the one who keeps blowing hot and cold, saying and doing one thing before changing my mind. How can you trust me when I can't trust myself?"

Colton slid his hand to Ioan's cheek, turning his face so Colton could stare at him in the eye. "I do trust you. You were scared. I understand that. Maybe, at the time, I was pissed, but I know the reasons behind it. The long-distance thing is gone. That's no longer a factor in this. I'm not saying we won't have issues, but the one holding you back the most is irrelevant now. I trust you to tell me when you're having issues with our relationship."

Ioan's expression was pensive, and Colton was worried he wouldn't believe him. There was no one who could change Ioan's mind. Ioan had to decide this for himself.

"Okay," Ioan muttered, sliding closer.

Colton swallowed hard. "Okay what?" His voice sounded strangled.

Ioan moved quickly, straddling Colton's lap and wrapping his arms around Colton's neck. "*Okay.*" Ioan's lips covered his in a soft kiss before he pulled back and smiled. "Best Christmas gift ever."

Colton threw his head back and laughed. "I agree." He clutched Ioan's back, not wanting too much space between them. "Do you have room for one more at your Christmas table?"

"I have room for one more at every mealtime."

Threading his fingers through Ioan's tousled black hair, Colton used his other hand to trace his features, smoothing a finger down his strong nose and across his full lips. This close, he could see the imperfections of Ioan's skin, but it added to his beauty, didn't diminish it. As Colton's fingertips slid over his jaw, he leaned closer. Ioan removed the distance completely, taking Colton's mouth in a deliciously hard and deep kiss when Colton instinctively opened to him.

They spent several minutes reacquainting themselves with each other's mouths and bodies until Colton pulled back. Resting their foreheads together and breathing heavily, Colton said, "Can you get the fire going?"

Ioan squinted at him with glassy eyes. "Huh?"

Smiling, Colton indicated the fireplace. "Get a fire going. I want to fulfil a fantasy." He nipped at Ioan's bottom lip.

Ioan shook his head and blinked rapidly, probably trying to gather his thoughts. He climbed off Colton's lap on shaky legs and stumbled over to the fire. While Ioan fiddled around, Colton grabbed the blanket off the back of the sofa and laid it on the floor—it would protect them a little from carpet burns. The hiss of the gas fire filled the room, and as Ioan stood in front of him, the flickering flames danced shadows across Ioan's face. Despite it being the middle of the day, the sky was overcast, allowing them the illusion of it being later.

Colton's hands lifted Ioan's shirt over his head and threw it behind him, his own following quickly after. He skimmed his hands down Ioan's smooth chest, falling to his knees when he reached the waistband of his trousers. Pulling the trousers down, he pressed a kiss to Ioan's stomach as Ioan stepped out of them. Colton scraped his fingernails around Ioan's sides to his back, causing him to squirm and laugh, but when Colton nibbled on his abs, the giggles became moans.

The hard length of Ioan pushed against Colton's chest as he held Ioan close, caressing every inch of skin Colton could reach. Ioan gripped Colton's head and pulled him away, leaning down to fuse their lips in an impatient gesture, then dropped to his knees. Their lips bit and nipped, alternately sipping and inhaling the other.

"God, more!" Ioan cried as they broke away to breathe.

Colton manoeuvred Ioan until he was lying on his back with Colton braced above him. Their gazes locked, and Colton felt his pulse increase further. He leaned down on his elbows, caging Ioan until there was only a millimetre of space between them. Colton knew what he wanted to say, but it was too early.

He kissed Ioan briefly, then kissed, licked and nibbled his way down Ioan's body. When he reached Ioan's waistband, he mouthed the tip peeking over the edge and pulled the boxers down, revealing the mouth-watering sight of a large, aroused cock. Ioan helped him get rid of his underwear, then spread his legs to allow Colton room.

Sparing a quick glance at Ioan's face, Colton licked up the underside of Ioan's dick before using his fingers to bring the hard length towards him. Eyes seeking out Ioan's, Colton sucked in the tip, watching Ioan's reactions. At least he did until he tasted him, then his whole focus narrowed in on the cock in his mouth. Ioan groaned as Colton sucked and swallowed him, thrusting his hips to get more. Colton pulled off, gasping, crawling up Ioan's body to kiss him.

Ioan's legs wrapped around him, then dropped off again. He pushed Colton's trousers and briefs down, freeing Colton's shaft. Colton kicked off the offending material and lowered his hips to Ioan's, moaning as their cocks came into contact.

"Fuck me, Colton," Ioan pleaded when their mouths parted.

Colton froze, dropping his head on Ioan's collarbone. "Lube and condoms are upstairs, aren't they?"

"No. In the side table." Colton raised his eyebrows, and Ioan blushed. "I remembered you saying you wanted this before..." he trailed off with a shrug.

Colton couldn't help it. He slammed his mouth back on Ioan's, licking inside while holding him still. When he pulled away, they were breathing hard again. Colton crawled forward to reach to the drawer, gasping as Ioan wrapped his fingers around Colton's dick. He barely felt it when he grabbed the items and dropped them next to Ioan, unable to move away from the pleasure Ioan was inflicting. Colton braced an arm on the sofa cushion as he drove his cock faster and harder through Ioan's grip.

"Oh, fuck. Stop, Ioan." Colton felt the sweat dripping down his face from withholding his climax, and he knew he needed to be inside Ioan. Now.

He moved back down until he was kneeling between Ioan's legs again, then squirted some lube on his fingers. Circling Ioan's hole, Colton waited until Ioan relaxed slightly before pressing in. He prepped Ioan as quickly and thoroughly as he could, watching as Ioan squirmed beneath him.

"Oh, god, now!" Ioan encircled his own shaft, squeezing the base hard.

Colton rolled on the condom, spreading lube generously, before bracing himself over Ioan once more. Taking his dick in his hand, he held it at Ioan's entrance. "You ready?" he croaked.

"Yes, fuck, yes!" Ioan's nails dug into Colton's shoulders with a bite of pain that Colton didn't mind at all.

Colton pushed forward steadily until he was fully seated. Pausing briefly, he checked Ioan's expression before withdrawing, a hiss leaving through his gritted teeth at the tingling rushing around his body. He kept his rhythm slow but constant until Ioan was writhing and gripping the blanket. Sweat beading on his skin, he rose to his knees and grasped hold of Ioan's hips. Using his hands and hips in tandem, he pulled Ioan towards him as he shoved his pelvis forward.

"Oh, fuck! Yes! Ah!" Ioan gasped, eyes glassy and wet.

Colton felt the tell-tale tingle at the base of his spine. "Jesus, Ioan. Come for me, sweetheart. Come for me!"

Ioan circled his cock, stroking fast and twisting at the top as Colton watched, flicking his gaze between Ioan's face and cock. "Shit!" Ioan's cock released, and the sight sent Colton over the edge. Clutching Ioan's hips tight to him, Colton dropped his head back and groaned as he climaxed.

When the orgasm finally released him from its

clutches, he pulled out and dropped to Ioan's side, resting an arm over his face.

Ioan linked their fingers together, and after Colton rose to grab a cloth, they lay there for a short time, tangled together in front of the fire.

"So, did it fulfil your dreams?" Ioan whispered from where his head was resting on Colton's chest.

"And more."

Ioan snuggled closer, and Colton caressed his upper arm.

"We need to move to the bed." Colton knew they couldn't leave the fire going all night—or all day, he had no clue what time it was—but he didn't really want to break the spell.

"In a minute."

In a minute ended up being a couple of hours later, after they'd had a nap. Ioan woke Colton up with his mouth, then they switched off the fire and ducked into the shower. Once they were semi-presentable, they made dinner.

"Are you going to come with me to see Mom tomorrow?" Colton took a huge mouthful of the lasagne they'd made.

"Of course! I mean, if that's okay?" Ioan's face flushed faintly pink.

"Definitely okay. Would you like to come with us to Uncle Brian's, too? It will be a bit crazy."

"If you want me there, I'm happy to come."

"I need to share my news with them." Colton grinned as he ate.

"I bet they'll love having you so close."

"I wonder how many times I'll be roped into babysitting now that I'm here?" Colton chuckled. "If I do, you're with me. No excuses."

"Deal." Ioan paused. "We can go and visit my dad at some point. I'll have to check with him to see when he's not busy."

"Whenever you want to." Colton covered Ioan's hand with his own, and Ioan turned his palm up so they could thread their fingers.

"Shall we go and see your Mom?" Ioan asked when they'd finished and had cleaned up the kitchen.

"Are you sure?"

"Yeah, come on. Let's go visit, then we can come back here and…" Ioan left the sentence hanging, but his raised eyebrows gave away his thoughts.

Colton laughed. "Sounds like a plan. I'll need to swing by the hotel to grab some clothes on the way back."

"How about we get a taxi to the nursing home, then we can get one to your hotel after. We can grab all your things in one go." Ioan bit his lip.

Colton cupped his face. "Are you sure?" he asked again.

"Never more sure of anything."

Colton leaned down and covered Ioan's mouth with his own. Their kiss was slow and explorative, leisurely and soft. When Colton pulled away, he dropped a kiss on Ioan's nose then forehead before stepping back.

"Let's go, then." He held out his hand, and when their fingers laced together, Colton's body relaxed.

CHAPTER SIXTEEN

IOAN

2021

"If you could put that over there, please." Ioan pointed to the corner of the room where an empty table stood. He checked another task off his clipboard list and ran his eyes down for the items still to be completed. He was working Christmas again this year, but only part of it. He had agreed to work Christmas Eve and the first half of Christmas Day after discussing it with Colton. Together, they decided that because Ioan was one of the few members of staff who had no children, it would be good for him to allow others to spend the morning with their family, and then in the afternoon, he would meet them at Uncle Brian's for a late lunch.

Laura had promised he would not have to cover for everyone every year, so next year he could have some time off. It was a fair trade and one neither he nor Colton minded.

It also meant that because he was there, he was directing the decorating and organisation of the hall to get it ready for their Christmas meal. Ioan was concerned, though. Everything was going surprisingly well. He frowned. Something always went wrong, but he had no idea what could, and it worried him. He didn't like surprises. Not those kinds, anyway.

"Thanks, Matthew," he said distractedly as the delivery guy left Ioan alone in the large room.

His thoughts turned to that morning in bed. He'd woken to Colton snuggling close and leaving kisses all over his neck and shoulders. One thing had led to another, as always, and Ioan had nearly been late for work. Before he'd left, Colton had given him a small blue box wrapped with a bow. It was the twenty-fourth little gift Colton had given him, and Ioan had been overwhelmed. Nestled inside was a wooden owl-shaped figure, one of Ioan's favourite animals.

After kissing Colton in thanks, he'd hurried over to the glass cabinet and placed it with the others he had. There were so many in there now, he would probably have to buy a new unit soon, but each and every one of them had some sort of meaning.

Colton was still woodworking. In fact, he had joined forces with Zak to create a sustainable business for them both. Zak had taught Colton what he knew and vice versa. Their business had grown exponentially. They were each capable of doing the other person's job, but they preferred to stay within their own niches when possible: Zak with his larger custom-made furniture items, Colton with his smaller custom-made trinkets.

A small smile played on Ioan's lips as he thought back over the previous year. Colton had checked out many houses after the new year, but nothing seemed to fit. Ioan took it as a sign and told Colton to stop being stupid and just stay with Ioan indefinitely. It was one of the first arguments they'd had, but eventually, they calmed down enough to rationally think it through. After sitting down and working through their finances and different scenarios, Colton agreed to stay. He'd admitted afterwards that he'd wanted to stay anyway but hadn't wanted to put pressure on Ioan.

Ioan chuckled and shook his head.

"Anything I can do to help?"

Ioan jumped and clutched his chest. "Jesus! Don't sneak up on me."

Colton laughed and wrapped his arms around Ioan, nuzzling his face into Ioan's neck. "Sorry. I thought you'd heard me."

Ioan leaned back into Colton's chest, closing his eyes in contentment. "How's Mum?" Rose had invited Ioan to call her Mum a few months ago, even though they were not married or even engaged. Ioan had triple-checked that it was okay with everyone before he finally agreed.

"Not so good. She started going downhill about an hour ago, so Marie is with her for a bit. She told me to have a breather."

Ioan turned in Colton's arms and slid his hands around his waist. "She'll be back to normal before you know it."

"Before tomorrow?" Colton raised his eyebrows in

question, though he already knew the answer Ioan would provide.

"Hopefully." Ioan could not give Colton a definite answer. No one could. Rose's body would do what it needed to do, whether it took several hours or several days.

They stayed wrapped up in each other for a few minutes before Colton pulled away. "Put me to work."

Ioan shook his head, then paused. "Why don't you go to Sweet Tooth and grab some cakes. Only for the staff, the residents already have something."

"Alright. I'll call a cab."

"Do you want to take the bike?"

"No. It's probably best that I don't. I know I've passed my test and everything, but having cakes on the back of it will worry the hell out of me."

Ioan chuckled. Colton had decided earlier in the year that he wanted to learn how to ride a motorbike, so they'd arranged lessons, and he'd passed his test two months ago. Colton was not planning on buying himself a bike yet, but he would eventually. He preferred to cycle to Zak's house whenever he was working.

"I'm sure they would be fine, but whatever you'd prefer."

Colton dragged Ioan's head close enough to kiss, then let go just as abruptly. "I'll be back soon."

"Say hi to everyone for me."

A lot had changed over the past year, but also some things had stayed the same. It was as if Colton had seamlessly slid into Ioan's life without a ripple of disquiet. Even Ioan's dad liked him. Ioan had expected some resistance from his dad, but there'd been nothing at all. Not that they'd seen him much, as per usual.

Ioan brushed his thoughts aside and focused on the job at hand. He placed his clipboard on a table and strode over to the stack of red and green tablecloths with white trim. Lifting one, he unfolded and laid it over a table, repeating until each table had been covered. That little bit of festive colour brightened up the room. By the time his shift was over, the dining hall had been transformed into a winter wonderland ready for Christmas lunch the following day, and Ioan's mood had significantly improved.

"You really are in a good mood tonight," Colton observed when they entered the house.

"It's Christmas. What do you expect?" Ioan shrugged.

"I know, sweetheart. Your new favourite time of year."

"It is. Right, I'm going for a shower. I need to be presentable for the party."

Colton slapped his ass as he shuffled past, and Ioan grinned. "Go on before I join you and we never get there."

"We will get there no matter what…there is so much to celebrate this year."

Smiling, Colton agreed.

Ioan hurried through his shower and dressed in dark jeans and an emerald green shirt, just as Colton entered the bedroom bare-chested. Ioan quickly swung away.

"What?"

"I'm not looking at you because if I do, we won't get

there! Hurry up and get changed. I'll meet you downstairs." He almost ran out of the room, pulse racing. Ioan wanted nothing more than to throw Colton down on the bed and have his way with him, but he really did want to go and see everyone at Crush. They had become close friends, and so many things had changed in just these last few weeks.

"Okay, I'm ready." Colton was pouting, Ioan could tell from the tone of his voice.

"Great. Taxi's here already. Let's go!" Ioan grabbed his hand and dragged him to the door. They bundled into their coats, locked the door behind them and climbed into the vehicle.

Entering the brightly lit bar, they took off their coats and elbowed their way through the crowds to the table the group usually sat at. When Ioan saw them, he grinned. It looked like most of the crew had managed to get there. After greeting everyone, they sat down, Colton wrapping his arm around Ioan's shoulders.

"How is Sean and Asher doing?" Ioan asked Max. Sean and Asher had gotten married two weeks ago, and then, while Asher's friend looked after his niece, went off on their honeymoon. Halfway through their trip, they had received a call that there was a child waiting to be fostered, and they were asked if they would be able to take him. They'd agreed immediately and raced home.

"They're doing alright. Maddox is very quiet, but Janie seems to have taken a liking to him. I don't know if Maddox is happy about that or not." Max chuckled.

"I bet that was a shock for them."

Max grinned. "Definitely. They hadn't expected to

have the opportunity with a child so quickly. Must be fate."

"Even better that Janie likes him. I couldn't imagine how many problems it might cause if there was any animosity between them."

"They're both pretty laid back now, so I'm sure they'd manage no matter what."

Ioan agreed.

"Would you like to have kids one day," Colton whispered in his ear.

A shiver ran through his body at the feel of his breath on his skin. Turning his face and lowering his voice, Ioan said, "I would love to have kids. What about you?" It was something that hadn't come up in discussion, yet surprisingly.

"The more, the merrier."

Ioan gazed at Colton with a small smile. "Good to know."

"Hey, Colton, Ioan. How're things?"

Tom, the manager of Crush, crouched next to them. Colton had known Tom for many years, from when he'd visited each Christmas, but Ioan had only just really started getting to know him. He and his wife, Ginny, had two beautiful children, one of whom had just had her third birthday.

"Hi, Tom. Did Kayleigh enjoy her birthday?" Colton asked with a gleam in his eye.

Tom narrowed his gaze on Colton. "It would've been absolutely perfect had it not been for the drum kit someone bought her." Tom sighed, though Ioan could see he wasn't truly bothered. "We've heard nothing but bass and cymbals for the last two days."

"Sorry," Colton said, sounding far from apologetic.

"Hmm. Are you both coming to the New Year's party?"

They both nodded. "Definitely."

"Good." Tom stood, clapping Colton on the shoulder. "Enjoy your night."

Ioan rested back against Colton's chest again, closing his eyes and enjoying the sounds all around him.

"Are you happy?"

Ioan opened his eyes, looking at Colton. He cupped Colton's jaw, bringing him closer. "Perfectly happy." He touched their lips together, licking along Colton's bottom lip to request entry before deepening the kiss.

Something bumped his face, and he pulled away, turning to see what it was. A wadded-up napkin laid on the table in front of him, and he narrowed his eyes at the occupants. Seeing Zak grinning, Ioan threw it back with a laugh.

"Stop cockblocking me!" Colton growled, pulling Ioan back into his arms.

"Like you're never going to get cock again." Zak rolled his eyes.

"He might refuse, you never know," Colton argued.

"*He* is right here, you know," Ioan deadpanned.

"Sorry, sweetheart." Colton nuzzled into his neck, and Ioan tilted his head to give him better access.

The next thing they knew, they were being pelted by napkin after napkin. When the ammunition ran out, Ioan held his ribs, trying to stop them from hurting due to how much he'd been laughing.

"How come…only we got…that treatment? What…about them?" he wheezed, pointing at Trent and Max, whose tongues were in each other's mouth.

"They will. When they least expect it." Ethan winked.

"You better collect all these napkins up then; you're going to need them."

Ioan finally reached Uncle Brian's house at two the following afternoon. He knew he would've missed the initial Christmas gift opening, but he didn't mind. Spending the afternoon relaxing with Colton's family was more than enough for him.

He knocked on the door, then entered as he'd been told to do. Unzipping his coat, he hung it up on the coat rack and slipped off his wet shoes. The weather, although mild, was very wet, but it was better than snow.

Venturing into the living room, he saw a lot of people sitting or lying around the room while some smaller children played with toys. Not wanting to disturb the semi-quiet, he walked softly to the kitchen, hearing voices and laughter the closer he got. Upon entering, he saw Brian setting the table, Rose pouring drinks, Mary manning the stove, and Colton stood by the sink, peeling potatoes.

Rose saw him first. "Ioan! You made it!" Despite going downhill the previous day, she had woken up that morning back to her normal self, much to his relief. He hadn't wanted Colton to miss out on the family celebration. Rose enfolded him in her arms. "Merry Christmas, Ioan."

"Merry Christmas, Mum."

His gaze flicked over her shoulder to where Colton was, waiting for him. Ioan made him wait, though. He shook hands with Brian and hugged Mary before standing in front of his boyfriend.

"Hey."

"Merry Christmas, Colton." They'd seen each other that morning, but Ioan had the early shift and needed to be at the nursing home by 6 a.m. It meant they hadn't spent much time together.

Colton embraced him, tucking his face into Ioan's neck as always. "I missed you," he whispered.

"Missed you, too."

"Go on, you two. Out you go. Send Katrina in, will you?" Mary waved them away with a smile.

After doing her bidding, they settled on the sofa in the conservatory, listening to the rain on the roof. Ioan had his legs over Colton's lap and his head resting on his shoulder.

"Can I tell you a secret?" Colton asked.

Ioan lifted his head, frowning. "Of course, you can. Is everything okay?"

Colton nodded, a serious look on his face. "You mean everything to me. It doesn't matter where you go, I will always follow. Do you know why?"

Ioan shook his head, unable to talk through the lump in his throat and the tears threatening to overflow.

"Because *you* are my home. Home is not a place. It's you. I love you so much."

Ioan lost his battle with his tears, and as they streamed down his face, he pulled Colton in for a fast, frenzied kiss. When he pulled away, he said, "I love you, too."

"Oi! Geppetto! Stop swapping saliva and get your ass in here to greet your guests. I didn't fly three thousand miles to see you kiss someone."

Dani's voice had Colton going still. Ioan hadn't told him of the *other* Christmas gift he'd gotten him. It had taken some figuring out, but Dani had finally managed to get on a plane with Jimmy and his girlfriend, Vanessa.

Colton beamed at him, swooped in for another kiss, then lifted Ioan up, helping him stand before grabbing his hand and rushing through the house.

Colton let go and pulled Dani and Jimmy into a hug. Whispered words were exchanged, but Ioan was happy to be left out at the moment. This was something Colton needed, something he didn't think he would be able to have. Ioan was glad he'd been able to do this for him.

He'd do anything for the love of his life. Anything.

Next in the series: Life Support
https://readerlinks.com/l/1588292

Would you like to read from the beginning of the series?
Pick up First Kiss!!
https://readerlinks.com/l/1566650

Sign up to my newsletter and receive a free short story
http://www.elouiseeast.com/newsletter

Could I ask you to leave a review, please? They are so
important to authors, not only because they allow other
readers to decide whether they will like the book or not,
but because it will help me grow as an author and
provide you with more books.
https://smarturl.it/ACFCReviewLink

Thank you!

I am a bestselling author of contemporary MM romance. I write a variety of themes: sweet and fluffy to high angst to taboo, but there is a huge nod in the direction of friendships being integral to each character's experience. I write books that are emotionally realistic, even if liberties are taken with other aspects of my stories.

Reading and writing have always been a part of my life, although my debut book wasn't published until July 2019, when I was 36 years old. My experience has come from reading thousands of books over the years and being a perfectionist when it comes to trying to make things right. I live in the centre of the UK with my two children, who make life worth living, keep me (in)sane and make me laugh. I love Zumba, yoga and walking, all things that can be done alone as I am very introverted.

Stalk me here… ;-)
WEBSITE: https://elouiseeast.com/
NEWSLETTER: https://elouiseeast.com/newsletter
LINKTREE: https://linktr.ee/elouiseeastauthor

BOOKS BY ELOUISE EAST

<u>CRUSH SERIES</u>

First Kiss

Instant Desire

Primary Seduction

Deep Down

A Crush for Christmas

Life Support

Covert Strength

Love Scene

Lawful Attraction

<u>JUST A LITTLE CRUSH</u>

Star-Crossed

He's Behind You

A Special Love (newsletter story)

<u>DADDY</u>

Love Me, Daddy

Soothe Me, Daddy

Spoil Me, Daddy

<u>DARK & DIVERGENT</u>

A Biker Make Three

Forbidden Temptation

Too Many Secrets

<u>CHARMED</u>

Treehouse Whispers

Rhythm Inside (Heard it in a Love Song Anthology)